In the City of Love's Sleep

LAVINIA GREENLAW

ff

FABER & FABER

First published in 2018
by Faber & Faber Limited
Bloomsbury House
74–77 Great Russell Street
London WC1B 3DA
This paperback edition published in 2019

Typeset by Typo•glyphix
Printed in the UK by CPI Group (UK) Ltd, Croydon, CR0 4YY

A CIP record for this book
is available from the British Library

ISBN 978–0–571–33763–7

2 4 6 8 10 9 7 5 3 1

to Lesley Henshaw and Franny Bennett
– friends of almost forty years

Pray then in your most brilliant lonely hour
That, reunited, we may learn forever
To keep the sun between ourselves and love.

from 'Venus', Malcolm Lowry

yes

Imagine a woman running. The long corridor is dark except for the red blips of smoke detectors and the green vapour of low-level after-hours lighting. She slams her raised hands into each set of fire doors and pushes hard so they flap behind her as if urging someone to follow her. Is someone following her? She takes the stairs two and then three at a time. These are the back stairs. They're concrete worn to slipperiness and she stumbles, bangs her knee, gets up and keeps running.

She reaches her office door but her keys – where are her keys? She pushes a hand into her bag but her fingers can't make sense of anything, they're not fingers at all, and so she shakes the bag, hears a clink, pushes her hand through it again and still can't find them. Is someone coming? She tips the bag onto the floor, grabs the keys, rushes in and stands there, against the wall, trying to catch her breath. She watches the open door. Nothing happens.

There was no touch, only the thought of it, not even a thought, less than thought. Her body was responding to – what? Even now, minutes after their conversation, she has no clear idea of what he looks like. When they spoke she could not meet his gaze. If she were to see him tomorrow she might walk straight past him. But something about him – what? – has woken a part of her that she had forgotten and which is right now the part most defining and defined.

Where is he? She's watching the door even though she knows he won't appear. She doesn't want him to – or does she – and anyway who is he? A man she'd never met before who turned towards her while unbuttoning his coat. There was something about him she recognised so strongly that she had to stop herself reaching out her arms.

They happened to leave the cloakroom together and walked into the hall side by side before moving apart. She spoke to colleagues and acquaintances, and she waited. If you'd asked her what she was waiting for, she wouldn't have been able to say. She had not yet formed so much as a thought about him but moved and spoke as if knowing herself watched. At certain points she caught sight of him and her body told her that she knew him, only of course she didn't. She'd been reminded of something by the way he unbuttoned his coat. That was all. She waited.

Neither could later remember how their conversation began. It was a turning towards one another as natural as waking. Within minutes they were talking about their fathers, both architects, neither successful and both now dead. She asked him if he'd wanted to become one too, was it expected of him as it had been of her, and he laughed and said no, his family never thought him clever enough and anyway what interested him was cupboards and what people chose to put inside them. She came away with an impression of gentleness and complication that she later construed as warmth and depth. And while she couldn't describe his face, she would remember the pleasure of being unable to place him. Who was he?

She had been telling him about her work, how she too

2

was interested in small things, and then she was about to ask if he would like to – what? Come up to her office? Even though the reception was ending and there was someone who she could tell was waiting for him, standing at the boundary of her awareness. She took his card, said goodbye and walked off behind the row of banners and press boards, back through the darkened gallery, past the locomotives and rockets and on up to the small things – the jealousy glass, the cloud mirror, the merman – any of which she could have offered so as to have him follow her. And as she walked away she saw it all – that her body was ticking and had she asked and had he followed she would have done anything, so sharply did the space between them fall away. And so she ran.

One night long ago, before she knew anything much about anything, Iris met a man at a dinner. It was a formal occasion to which she'd been invited at the last minute by her employer because someone had dropped out. She knew no one and realised as soon as she got there that she was wrongly dressed. All this meant she was particularly grateful when the man next to her introduced himself warmly and confided that he didn't know anyone either except – he gestured down the table towards a tall woman with a plait of slate-and-silver hair – his wife. At that same moment his wife shook hands with the man who had just sat down beside her. *Oh!* Iris exclaimed, because she saw something in the wife's face: she was saying yes to this stranger as you can only say yes to someone who is saying yes to you. *Yes*, they were saying to each other. *Yes*.

We can say yes to a stranger without even slowing down as we pass by. This is not the yes of accepting something offered (nothing's been offered) but that of recognition. What is it we recognise? The stranger is rich in tension, both body and blank surface, never seen before and yet familiar. Some detail of proportion, tone, feature or gesture connects with a memory we may not even know we have and this is what we recognise.

It doesn't have to be a stranger. It could be someone you've known for years who was once the person who unbuttoned their coat, walked beside you into a room or sat next to you at dinner. There would have been a moment of yes but of the kind that is folded away. That kind of yes can settle beyond reach. Or it might keep a loose shape and be there every time you meet, and one day suddenly become so clear.

From time to time Iris has wondered what happened to the couple at that dinner. Back then she'd thought them too old for their flirtation to be anything more than good manners. The husband had persisted in talking to Iris, trying for minutes at a time not to look at his wife, only sooner or later his head would turn and his sentence trail off. Not once when Iris followed his gaze did she see his wife look back. The yes that she and the stranger were saying to one another was so strong that at the other end of that crowded table, they were terribly clear. The wife had turned her seat towards the stranger and remained fixed, her arm propped on the table, her hand holding a glass as if it were a divine attribute, that heavy slate-and-silver plait now brought forward, girlishly, over one shoulder. The stranger leant back and spread his arms as if to receive her, one disappearing along the back of her chair. At a certain point he left the table and Iris saw to her surprise that he looked much like the husband, who had just spilt his drink and so did not watch the stranger pass.

Did the wife carry home this encounter like a jewel slipped into her pocket, something she found in her hand now and then, turned over and let drop? Did her husband see after all that this woman was not just his wife but a creature of volition and mystery who might at any point reach past him? Or had he always known? Was whatever remained of her love for her husband demolished by that evening's strength and shine? If their marriage came to an end, we might say that it was always going to do so and that the stranger's attention only lit her discontent.

In adolescence, love is like a river urgently in need of direction. It might flow towards a horse, a superhero, a football player, a singer. These are love's rehearsals. One day the river flows towards someone who is real and there. This suggests that the feeling comes to us before the subject and yet that's not how it's experienced. A fifteen-year-old girl is struck by the boy who cycles past her window each evening. She is not struck by her love.

Only when it's over and she has discovered his ordinary nature, might she wonder. Probably not. She will go on experiencing the yes in herself and only when it has led to more than the gentle disappointment of the boy on the bicycle, to damage and pain, might she stop within it and say *I know what this is. I'm saying yes. That's all and it's nothing – memory, association, need, desire, nothing.*

Or she will look at the person she's chosen and remember the first time she saw them and how her whole self said yes and here they are in a life together. Perhaps that's what happened to the woman with the slate-and-silver plait and her stranger. In hindsight we call this love at first sight – when yes is met with yes and circumstances or propensities allow it to amplify unending.

follow

The man Iris watched unbuttoning his coat also finds him-self hard to place. The complication she saw in him is sadness. His wife died and such is his grief that he appears more alive when he feels less so. If he feels anything at all it is that life has become diagrammatic. There are steps and he takes them.

At forty he is six years younger than Iris, although the tentativeness with which he moves through the world makes him appear well-established in middle age. He has his Mauritian father's Arab father's name, Raif, which his parents chose as his other, Irish, grandfather was called Ralph. Most assume it is an alternative spelling and he does not correct them.

Raif grew up in a town on the south coast in a street between the golf course and the sea wall. He teaches at one of the dozen universities in the city. His subject is the his-tory of science and he was on the museum's guest list because he once wrote a book about curiosity cabinets. It was published ten years ago and has now disappeared so completely that he's not even sure he owns a copy. He didn't notice Iris when he was taking off his coat but he was conscious of the moment they passed through the entrance to the hall. Something formulated itself as if they briefly entered a dance. This remained with Raif throughout the party and drew him to her.

Had they met before? Iris was a powerful presence though he could not yet say why. She was small and simply dressed but she was quite definite and unusually still. In the sea of the room, she appeared as dry land. In the end she turned and there he was and they started talking as if someone had just introduced them. He found that he wanted to tell her things and gave extensive answers to her questions until they both caught up with what was happening, something was moving too fast, and the conversation faltered. Iris said she must leave. Raif gave her his card but she did not reciprocate or even say thank you as she hurried away.

His colleague Rosa came over and slipped her arm through his. (In what way did she want to say he belonged to her?) She suggested they go for a drink. *For ten years I was a married man*, he pondered, *and now I'm not and I don't know what this means.* This thought has become a habit and a place to rest. *I don't know what this means.*

As soon as they were in the street, Rosa pulled out her phone and started tapping through her messages. Raif walked beside her as she made a call and, still talking, gestured towards a sign that said Bar. Raif nodded his agreement and they followed the sign down into a basement.

The table was small and the music loud. They had to work to keep their legs from touching and lean forward so as to hear one another. Their mouths almost brushed when they spoke. What was he thinking? Rosa was chatting in a distracted way that made clear this meant nothing. They'd worked together for years and yet now she was so close that he was overcome by dangerous detail: her open mouth, the three studs in one ear, her pea-green finger-nails and—

Rosa was talking. She had taken his hand.

Raif.

He moved his fingers. Did he really just stroke her wrist? She pulled her hand away.

It's a long process, she was saying, but don't *use* it. Two years is long enough.

Use what? What for? She stood up and bent to kiss his cheek. This time her proximity was motherly. Had she turned something off or had he? He pretended he wanted to stay and have another drink and watched her go. He had nearly done something very stupid. What had he been thinking? *I don't know what this means.*

He's crossing the city, surprised to realise that it's not all that late and that other people are just starting out on their evenings. The streets are still relaxed, the pubs crowded but orderly. It is early summer, the time of year when the city offers its gentlest possibilities. A chance for things to unfold at their own pace and yet Raif hurries home. It's only ten o'clock and so much has happened. He's exhausted.

Back in his flat he wants to stop thinking about Rosa (or is it Iris who has disturbed him so?). Eventually he phones Helen, the woman he's been seeing for a while. At first Raif contacted her whenever he wanted to do the kind of thing you do with someone else. They would go to a film or a concert and wake up together and she'd suggest ways of filling the day that meant leaving the house and being in

9

the world. He's not good at such things on his own. His inertia is habit as much as grief. Women perceive him as deep and men as slow.

He asks Helen to come over and she hesitates because she has an audition in the morning and then says yes. Raif lets her in, offers her a glass of wine and talks about how tired he is. They sit for a few more minutes and then he gets up and says, as if to no one in particular, that he needs to go to bed. Helen has already taken her overnight bag upstairs. She goes to the bathroom and applies cream to her face with concentrated little dabs that Raif finds annoying. He reaches for his toothbrush and Helen steps aside.

Raif climbs into bed as if alone and reads the paper while Helen gets undressed. He doesn't look up as she slips off the underwear she changed into when he rang and stuffs it into her bag. She lies neatly beside him. Raif puts down the paper, turns out the light and places his hand between her legs. She waits but his hand is still.

Three hours later Raif starts to sob and Helen wakes him. He kisses her deeply, pressing his head against hers. She takes her cues from him as they try together to make him come but he is medicated as well as exhausted and this is like dragging up an anchor. Eventually he lifts Helen's face to his.

I'm sorry.

It's fine.

I'm sorry that I can't—

You're tired.

That I can't offer you more.

I'm fine, she says, and just as he starts to drift off she adds, It'll soon be a year.

You mean two.

Two? Oh. I didn't mean . . . I meant—

Two years. Since my wife died.

I meant us. Helen's voice has become repellently small. Almost a year since the start of us.

She knows he's not listening and wonders why she brought it up. It's not something she's thought about before but there have been enough nights like this for her to start to wonder what she's doing, what this is. He is not unfolding. If anything, tonight, he is more tightly folded than he has been before.

Raif spoke to Iris for a matter of minutes. What does he see in her? What he needs to. He sleeps and wakes and what comes to mind is a woman turning away. He follows her.

At nine o'clock, Iris leaves the museum and walks towards the station. The great blank doors of this street of institutions are closed. The drifts of children have gone. The tourists, amiable and regular, have gone. Now there are students returning to their dilapidated residences and cleaners going to work. Iris is wearing her summer clothes because it is the end of May and an old tweed coat because it has been cold for weeks and she is slow to make such adjustments. In her loose dress and large coat, with her short hair, she might look childish were her bearing not so considered.

Is this really summer? The people of the city rush through any scattering of fine days impatient for the season to reach its height. When time stretches out hot and dry, and we have what we wanted, we grow anxious for change. If such weather persists, the city issues warnings. Teams stationed at major intersections hand out sponsored bottles of water. All this we have come to expect but how do we prepare ourselves now that the sun blazes for a week in November and rain falls from February to June?

When Iris reaches the station she keeps walking, south through the crescents and squares towards the river. These streets are lit differently. Discreet pools of lamplight seem to shy away from the houses. Iris doesn't belong here. Ordinarily she would despise the locked communal gardens and silky cars. But tonight it's somewhere that's letting her pass unnoticed.

She will not think of this evening's encounter but her body is full of it and what she will not say, even to herself, is being processed in slow detonation. As long as she puts no words to it, she can allow herself to feel this pleasurable shock. It is not something we get to decide on or choose. It's body and memory working in a way that makes it impossible to tell one from the other. At twenty-six Iris would have held on or let go without equivocation. Even at thirty-six, that part of her was regularly woken. But she is forty-six and this encounter feels so unfamiliar that she is like herself at sixteen.

When she gets home her husband has already put on his coat. They stand on the doorstep and make arrangements for the coming week. There's nothing more to say but David makes no move to leave.

So, he says.

So?

She knows what he's talking about.

You said you'd decide.

Did I.

He reaches out his hand and she flinches.

For fuck's sake, Iris.

That morning she'd been woken at five by her daughters and for once saw them as what they were: ten and almost twelve years old and stretched to the limits of childhood.

Dad's not well, said Lou.

Since the separation Lou has assumed charge of whatever she can and Kate has become her shadow.

Your father's tired, Iris replied. We all are. What the hell time is this?

Kate's face was pleading with her mother not to be cross.

It's morning, technically, said Lou.

And I was asleep, technically.

Lou's voice was getting more emphatic.

He might have an episode.

What makes you think that?

He told us, rushed out Kate. He was cooking our pasta and he had to lie down so we—

Lou jabbed her with an elbow.

What did he say? Iris asked.

Kate was shaking her head so theatrically that Iris smiled.

It's not funny! Lou screamed it, really screamed.

Iris took her in her arms while Kate did her best to hold them both and said the things that Iris would usually say, which sounded so bleak and fake that Iris couldn't stand to hear them.

The situation simplified into her daughters' pain and what she could do to relieve it. She struggled with sleepless children, violent mornings, the lists and costs and machinery of life, which she now had to keep up with on her own. The house was falling down. The house would have to be sold. David couldn't go on living in his sister's spare room forever. But that was this morning and since then she's been reminded of something.

David is still standing on the doorstep.

Iris. You said you'd decide.

It occurs to her that they've started using each other's names. As if pushing each other away. She's heard the girls, up in their room, referring to them as David and Iris too. Is that what the children are doing? Pushing these troublesome parents away? She finds something to say.

The girls said you weren't well.

He shrugs and straightens up.

Nothing to worry about.

She knows he doesn't mean this but takes hold of it anyway.

That's good. It might be helpful if you reassured them.

What he feels now – the coldness of his wife, the loneliness of his illness, the severance from his daughters – moves so powerfully through him that he shudders. He reinforces his voice and is trying to think of something conciliatory to say when he notices. Her force is all inward. She is caught up.

Who are you fucking? He's grinning now so as not to cry.

14

Iris backs away. It's as if he watched her walk home, her body blaring excitement. It was obvious, wasn't it? She's become one of those women – giddy, flattered, thrown off course. The thrill running through her as if she were thirty-six, twenty-six, sixteen. And so she says what she says out of wanting to conceal this ridiculous self.

Not you, David.

He grabs at her as she pushes him out of the door and slams it shut. He bangs and shouts.

Who is he? Who is he?

When she looks up she sees her daughters on the landing. The next second they're not there. Did she invoke them to make her open the door and take him back?

The hall is quiet. David has gone. She sits on the stairs.

the bone skates

When Raif asked what she was working on, Iris told him about the bone skates recently excavated on the edge of the old city and thought to be almost a thousand years old. This morning's task is to assess them. She puts on gloves before lifting out each flat, narrow object. Eroded and compressed, they're still porous enough to absorb the slightest amount of grease from her fingers. She works in a room without windows but even this air is rich enough to cause harm.

Would it be harm or just more change? After all, the skates have been made and used and lost. They disappeared into centuries of clay and ice only to surface when the bulldozers started to claw away layers of the city in preparation for the new rail line which will run from east to west.

The skate Iris has selected for display is dark brown. It's a horse's cannon bone, the long bone beneath the knee. Compacted by the press of the body and worn down by the ice, it has lost its natural coarseness and taken on the polished grain of wood. The only evidence that it is a skate is the drilled holes through which a leather thong would have been threaded.

Her job is to fix things as they have been named. A museum object must communicate itself and so the skate will be put in place as a skate, not as part of a horse, or as bone, although all that will be explained in its caption. Iris has been trained to protect objects and to strengthen them without alteration while remaining aware that, in practice, this is something that cannot be done.

A thousand years ago the east wall of the city was met by a waterlogged moor. When it froze over in winter, young men would polish the shinbones of cattle, tie them to their feet and *play upon the yce*. Further north this wasn't play but the only way to travel. A long narrow lake which had been dark water all summer froze over and became a way to fly through the forest. *Some tye bones to their feete, and under their heeles, and shoving themselves by a little picked staffe, doe slide as swiftly as a birde flyeth in the aire, or an arrow out of a crossbow.*

Like many of the objects that interest Iris most, these skates are not attractive. Bone, which looks so rosy and lithe when cut from the body, dries into something coarse and dull. Is it animal? Mineral? The thing we're strung upon is the part of us that appears least alive.

the only thing to do

When they meet for the third time, Raif will tell Iris that he has a broken heart. He is telling the truth – his heart finds it difficult to cohere. He will never know what it was about Liis that made his heart become a single solid part of him but that was her effect. He married her in order to save her but he would have married her anyway because he was in love.

Raif had been finishing his PhD. He was tense with sexual ambition that alarmed his otherwise cautious nature. Women started to pursue him and he allowed things to happen. If someone flirted he flirted back, and as he did not know how to calibrate this, he got into trouble. Relationships appeared to form without his having decided anything and ended the same way. He was helping at a conference at his university when he first saw Liis. She stood out because she was dressed like the company executive that it turned out she was.

Raif's experience has been that life, people and feelings surge and recede. It is in his nature to wait. Sooner or later a surface forms and he moves across it without much thought as to direction or consequence. But he rushed towards Liis. A series of meetings followed which he orchestrated as if they were stages in a ceremony. He felt as if he were skating madly on a frozen lake – leaps, reversals, figures of eight – which wasn't a bad feeling because, unbelievably, he could!

She was an American who turned out to be Estonian and whose English was extremely clear but left no residue. He rarely felt as if he'd gleaned or grasped anything from their conversations and he found this a relief. On the first night they spent together, he led her back to his tiny student room. She undressed and got into bed. He did the same. When it grew light he drew back the covers. She placed his hands where she wanted them to be and indicated what she required of him. He had never concentrated like this, never really looked. He stared at her perfect surfaces till she made a small sound and pulled him towards her.

Afterwards, he took his clothes into the bathroom, got dressed and waited in the corridor for her to appear. He couldn't afford to buy her breakfast in a cafe so he made tea and toast and, even though it was February, suggested they carry it outside and sit on a bench on the scrubby grass opposite. He wanted even breakfast to be an occasion. This was where Liis told him about New York.

Her father had been a diplomat during the Soviet era, high up and trusted to travel. When she was eighteen he'd asked permission to take her with him on a trip to New York. New York! Liis recalled the amazement she felt at the marble of the hotel foyer, the wrapped soaps, the towels, the elevator to the thirty-fifth floor, the colour and variety and quantity of everything. On the last day of her visit, when they were in the lobby and about to get a cab to the airport, her father turned to her and said that he was going to defect. She could go home and denounce him or she could stay in New York. She had a minute to decide.

At this point in the story Liis broke off, leaving Raif

hunting for a response. He knew no one whose life had involved anything on this scale. Was this a good or a bad thing for a father to have done? He offered something non-committal.

You stayed, I guess. Of course. I mean—

She was staring straight ahead, not looking at him or the trees or the sky or anything.

Of course.

What about your mother?

Liis shook her head.

Did you see her again?

Last summer. People were starting to go back and I thought—

What about your father? Did he go back with you?

He's dead.

So what happened last summer?

I saw my mother.

There was no emotion in her voice or tension in her body but he felt compelled to comfort her. He reached out and touched the back of her hand with the tips of his fingers.

Are you cold? he asked.

Not really.

But she shivered and pulled his arm around her.

He held her as tentatively as he always would in the years to come. They continued to sit on the bench for some time while Raif wondered what to say next and then realised he wasn't expected to say anything. How restful! He finished her story for himself, projecting onto the blankness of her lovely face all he could conjure of this drama.

A teenager in a hotel lobby trying to choose a future.

Life narrowing to a point at which you have to act. Such moments take us into a simple world of large gestures where the stakes are high and the dangers clear. Liis grew brighter and brighter. No wonder Raif fell in love.

A year after their wedding he'd been sitting with some students in a pub. One was talking about a trip he'd made to Estonia.

People got caught up in ways we can't imagine. Occupation by one side and then the other. The Soviet years. Unbelievable stories. I met this woman who had just come back for the first time since she was eighteen. Her father had been this high-up diplomat, completely trusted, and he'd gone to New York. He'd got permission to take one of his children with him.

When was this? asked Raif.

I don't know – the late eighties?

I mean when did you meet her?

When I was there last year. She and her husband were staying in the same hotel. A lovely woman but you could tell really sad . . .

Raif sat up very straight.

My wife is Estonian and she—

His voice had tightened and he was gripping his chair. Something was about to crash in and sweep him away. The boy who was talking barely looked up from his beer.

Your wife? Really? They're beautiful people but quite sad, right? Anyway, this woman, she was only eighteen, goes off to New York with her father, has a whale of a time—

I've heard this story before, said one of the others. Doesn't he defect?

That's right! I suppose she's famous or something.

What was her name? asked Raif.

Anja something. Anyway, on the last day of their trip they were waiting for the taxi to take them to the airport . . .

Raif would say nothing of this. He went home and lay down beside his wife as if he were lying down on the surface of the frozen lake over which he'd skated for so long.

a failed instrument

Iris is old enough to know that decisions, like the emotions behind them, have many components. It's a question of bringing things into balance, which is something she's good at. It is in her nature to be methodical, cautious and detached. Yet an encounter with a stranger has stopped her seeing through the decision she'd made to repair her family. While she hates to think she could be so easily redirected, she knows that meeting Raif is connected to how she now feels, which is in many small ways more ambitious and alive.

It's a dull weekend and her daughters are fractious. Everything they used to enjoy is boring. Iris wants to work on a report but she needs documents that she's left in the museum stores, a building to the far west of the city where she works part of most weeks.

The girls are slumped at either end of the sofa, sporadically kicking each other. Iris pushes herself between them.

Do you want to come into work with me?

She looks at Kate who looks at Lou who slumps further before she replies.

To see stuff? We've done that.

Kate strives to sound as weary as her sister.

We've seen everything.

You haven't seen where I work in the stores.

What's so interesting about the stores?

There are three times as many objects there as in the museum.

Lou considers this and then something occurs to her.

The stores – they're private, right?

Well, yes, in that the public don't have access.

So it's like a special area, where normal people can't go?

Yes. You need a special pass and special permission.

OK, then.

Bring your coats.

It's summer.

Bring your coats.

Lou and Kate have lived all their lives in the city and like everyone they know less of it than they think. They have their routes and destinations and take little notice of what lies between. There is the standard map of the city with its attractions and shops and monuments and the areas that everyone's heard of. And then there is a subtler map of places whose names are not so widely known and whose location most would find hard to define. These tend to be where the city is unsure of itself, where nothing is what it seems and where one thing abrades or opposes another and nothing coheres. It is in such a place that Lou and Kate now find themselves, and they are uncertain and intrigued.

The stores are located in a rambling building which was originally the headquarters of the national savings bank. At the turn of the twentieth century four thousand people sat here in rows, men and women in segregation, processing a hundred thousand items of correspondence a day. This was a place designed for people engaged in an abstract activity: the movement of money. Now it's almost empty of people and full of things.

Lou assesses the sooty brick, tired drainpipes and dingy foyer with a sharp up-and-down sweep of her eyes. This is how she is learning to manage any new encounter. You look at someone as if there's something wrong with them before they can look that way at you.

This doesn't look like stores, she says.

Kate takes her mother's hand as if Iris is the one who needs reassuring.

Mamma, she says. Can we see something now?

They follow Iris up stairs and along corridors. The warmth of the day drops away and they slip into their coats. They might be in a church, a hospital or a prison. There aren't many windows.

I don't like this air, says Kate. It's old.

Well this is a place full of old things, says Iris.

She starts their tour with a room full of votive objects. There are rows of clay wombs and phalluses, and rough figures with swollen bellies. The girls move solemnly from one case to the next, going through the act of looking, but these things are too small and vague to interest them.

Why aren't they arranged? asks Lou.

Because they're not on display.

The girls are used to museums as places where objects are either out of reach, behind glass or put into your hands. Here they move carefully and keep their distance. Kate sees a look on Iris's face that she thinks is disappointment.

Which is your favourite thing? she asks.

In the stores, objects are labelled only by number. The

magic of investment takes place in the museum galleries. Visitors stare at a lump of clay because a caption tells them how rare and important it is – where it was found, how long ago and what powers it has. Iris wishes people could experience the unlabelled object first: see it as a lump of clay and only after that as a way of reading the future.

She unlocks a cabinet, takes down a tray and explains that this particular lump of clay is a copy of a model of an animal's liver. The original, which is in another museum, is four thousand years old.

This is four thousand years old? asks Kate.

No, says Iris. This is a copy. But it is about a hundred.

What are all those marks? Kate is trying to be interested. Lou won't look.

Babylonian script, says Iris.

What's it say?

I don't know.

Then what's the point? says Lou.

They're a set of predictions. A priest would sacrifice an animal, cut out its liver and look for marks. And then he or she would look at the same place on the model and that would be the prediction. Like an oracle or a horoscope.

Did they kill the animal first or just cut out their liver? asks Kate.

Kate is trying hard to feel that this is something special but Lou is starting to need to say things more than she needs to protect her mother.

Why would a museum want a copy? she says.

To fill the gaps in a collection.

Even if it's not the real thing?

Iris hesitates and then tries to explain.

It's very hard to say that anything is the real thing. Everything turns out to be a version of something else or a version of an idea.

Am I a version? asks Kate.

I suppose so, says Iris. You're a version of me and Dad but you're also an original, yourself, the real and only thing.

Kate laughs with delight at this but Lou is rigid in her boredom.

Why are there so many of the same thing? she asks. Don't you need just one?

The man who collected all this didn't think so.

Her daughters aren't interested in what the collector might have thought. Iris wonders what else she can offer.

We have fifty dentist's chairs.

Lou shakes her head.

They're only dentist's chairs.

Yes, but there are fifty.

Kate puts herself between them and as if she were five rather than ten, she shouts: I want to see!

The museum has put two dentist's chairs on display in expensive mock-ups of surgeries of the relevant era. The chairs blend into their proper settings. Here, in the basement of the stores, huddled together alongside the iron lungs and radiography machines, they are perturbing.

The girls are impressed.

So much strange furniture, whispers Kate.

The basement is full of versions of beds, tables, cupboards and chairs. From plain wooden slats to a red velvet throne, leather, chrome, plastic and paintwork of a pale clinical green, they all have the same ambivalence. *Rest*, they say, but also *endure*.

For hundreds of years we have been finding new ways to enter and interfere with the body. Now, when we cut open a body or study its internal markings, all we can predict is why it isn't working, whether it will work again, and perhaps for how long.

That evening Iris's phone keeps ringing while she's watching television with the girls. It buzzes away on the table in front of them and all three can see David's name. Iris doesn't move. The fourth time he rings, Kate reaches out but Lou stops her. They copy their mother and concentrate on the programme. Iris pretends not to notice but she's horrified. When did the girls become these pale little diplomats? They're too young to have to be so careful.

Once they're in bed, she rings David.

They're are under such strain, she says. We should both try harder not to impose on them.

You want me to pretend not to be ill?

But you aren't ill, she wants to say, not most of the time. She says nothing.

You always said we should give them the facts, he says.

Shall we give them the facts about why you had to leave?

Because you were so angry all the time? I think they know that.

I never let them see my anger. Never.

As she says this, Iris feels something twist inside. David's

28

voice thins as he reaches for what might hurt her most.

You think you're so in control. I had to rescue you before we'd even said hello, remember?

That's not fair.

It's true, though, isn't it?

She notices that he's breathing strangely.

Are you drunk, David? You're drunk.

She's right. David lay down at lunchtime with a bottle of whisky. He wants to know who Iris is fucking and hates the fact that whatever is going on makes him want to fuck her too. But she doesn't want him or his body. Most of the time now he can't get it up and then there's the problem of continence. He can't get it up and he can't hold it in, while Iris is being transformed back into her old fuckable self. And someone else, not him, is making that happen.

He slams into her and she slams back, forgetting that his condition sometimes makes him slur his words just as it makes him shake and stumble and need to lie down. Iris despises herself as much as she despises David. They're two blunted and acid individuals who've discovered that it's easy to say the worst thing. They aren't adults in pain, they're monsters.

Iris and Max are wearing thick jackets as they stand in a chilly hallway in the stores making tea from a kettle on a shelf. The kitchen has been requisitioned. There are always more objects. Iris has been working with Max since before David's diagnosis. When they met she was the mother of two tiny girls, still blurred, with an erratic but charming husband. She and David struggled but they had the resilience that comes from believing that the struggle will end.

Iris's job this morning is to retrieve and prepare sections of nineteenth-century marine telegraph cable for a researcher visiting this afternoon. The cable is so frayed and corroded that she's anxious about moving it. She puts on gloves, lifts each tray from the shelf and places it on a trolley, which she wheels down the corridor to the lift. The lift is broken and the research room is two floors below. When she rings Max to ask for help, she sees that there's a message from David. She leaves it unread.

If an object has to be carried, an act that is fraught with risk, then it must be for as short a distance as possible. Only when Max is in position with another trolley one floor below does Iris pick up the first tray and walk down the stairs. Once every section has been safely transferred to the second trolley, they repeat the exercise and move down another floor. The lift won't be repaired for weeks.

When they reach the study room Iris reads the message from David: *Your anger sucked the joy out of their childhood. They learnt to creep round you. We all did. You're terrifying.* Iris is shaking because she believes that this might be true.

Is it from David? asks Max. Has he said no?

No to what?

Coming back. I thought—

I didn't ask him.

But you said you'd decided.

I hadn't.

You had.

I know. I mean I don't know. Anyway. No.

Iris does not like to be seen. She turns away from the gaze of her husband and her friends. She turned away from Raif as soon as he started to meet her eyes. This is her most characteristic gesture and it draws people towards her because they feel they can't quite see her. She has also for many years been turning away from herself.

Max suggests they go up onto the roof for a cigarette. There's a fire exit out through a window onto a series of spacious terraces punctuated by chimney pots, lightning conductors, aerials and ventilation units. Their view is into the sunset and the low line of the edge of the city. There are towers here too but they are neither valued nor protected. Their walls are cheap and their windows small.

Max, without looking at Iris, confronts her.

Do you think you can go on deciding?

I'm not aware of a deadline.

Nothing's going to happen to make things any clearer.

(Raif comes electrically to mind.)

Something can happen that has nothing to do with anything, Iris says, but it helps you see.

Max knows that she finds this kind of conversation difficult.

You mean like an augury? Did you see a miraculous image in the broken cable we've been hauling about all morning?

Iris doesn't laugh, which makes Max curious.

So what made you change your mind?

I don't know what it is or what it means but something's different. I suppose I've been waiting for a sign and it's as if there's been one and I've missed it.

The cable that Iris and Max carried so gently down the stairs had once been laid across the bed of the Atlantic. After a thousand miles of it was in place, it broke and had to be abandoned. Now that a hundred and fifty years have passed, these salvaged sections are no longer just part of a failed instrument but historical artefact. Over time, things pass from being common to obsolete to rare.

So much of what's displayed in the museum reflects discovery and progress but there have been many more inventions that didn't work or weren't adopted. Even so, these failures were a vital step. Eventually cables were laid that did not snap, telegraphs were sent, telephone wires followed, and the four thousand people who sat in this building processing letters were out of a job.

We make a mistake or take a wrong turn and if we're wise we build on it and so a path grows. It's like drawing a map out of precipices and dead ends.

who are you?

As you gather information about someone, you think you see them ever more clearly. Perhaps you'll never see them as clearly as at first meeting when the yes was said.

Iris types Raif's name into the search engine and then deletes it. She's like a girl who will only dare write the name of her crush in the sand when the tide is coming in. A girl who picks up a net and throws it towards the sea and as the net unfurls it keeps growing and instead of the three silver fish she wished for, she hauls in every sea creature that ever was: cloud after cloud of small matter, entire landscapes, things that thrash and things that glide, dazzle and stink. The more the girl pulls at the net the more gets cast up until she's surrounded by tall shadows and tiny details, thrash and glide, dazzle and stink, and she can only let go.

The three silver fish Iris wants to hold in her hands are enough information to give this man substance and presence. No more. She would say she's curious and that he's a potentially useful professional contact, more or less a colleague. Will she discover that he looks nothing like she remembers? (What does she remember?) She doesn't want to find herself poking around inside his life. (Is he married?)

Iris types his name again and deletes it but she needs to make a connection to compensate for the one that she has just denied herself. She needs to feel a thread being drawn. She types a different name.

She was eighteen, still new to the city and halfway through her first term at university. Though shy and uncertain in company, Iris was then sure of her heart. It said yes or no and she listened. She hadn't yet found those who would become lasting friends, and had gone alone to a number of events where she stood in a corner and smoked. At one of these she met a boy who looked like a boy from home in that he too buttoned his collar and flopped his hair over one eye. But this boy wore bad jeans and carried a rucksack which was not the same thing as the backpacks the art students affected. Iris was concerned with this kind of detail but she was also flattered by his blunt attention and was about to discover a capacity in herself to set detail aside.

This boy was refreshing. He wasn't studying art history, as she'd assumed, but engineering at a neighbouring college. She liked his smooth build, his sweet features. They danced without acknowledging that they were dancing together and he was good at that too. She'd gone back to his room, where they had straightforward sex during which he was efficient and polite. It was clear that it wouldn't be easy for them both to sleep in his single bed so she made her way back to her own.

He didn't get in touch but Iris was not the type to dwell on that. The next Saturday night she set out for the same club and saw him in the street just ahead of her with a group of friends. She was about to catch them up and say hello when they stopped to cross a busy junction and one of his friends, a tiny girl in black with backcombed blonde hair, stepped into the road just as a car swerved round the corner and he yelled *Jen!* The blonde stepped back and they all laughed and walked on.

Iris knew from the panic in his voice that Jen wasn't just a friend. She marched back to her room thinking that everyone she passed had seen this humiliation: her face light up when she saw him, her awkward acceleration and then his shout. *Jen.*

She went over and over this, not realising that she had little interest in either the engineer or the blonde. She was fascinated by her own acuity – that a girl had stepped out in front of a car and a boy had yelled a warning and from the tone of that single syllable, their relationship had been revealed to her. It was a good story, though she never told it. It didn't occur to her that she might have been wrong.

Some months later, after she'd kissed two more people and been to bed with one of them, she was happily alone listening to records and selecting postcards for the board above her desk when the engineer knocked at her door. He asked, quite formally, if she'd like to go for a drink and walked her some way to a backstreet pub. She remembers a brown, muted room.

Would you like a glass of brandy?

Yes, she said, not knowing whether she wanted one or not.

I wonder if they've got any lovage, he said. Have you ever drunk brandy and lovage? You haven't? It's a herb cordial. It's traditional.

35

He returned with two glasses of brandy. The pub didn't have lovage and this seemed to change his mood. They left as soon as they'd finished their drinks and he walked back slightly ahead of her.

Iris still can't imagine having such an effect on someone that they would knock on her door and then be unable to say why. Nor can she see this from the boy's perspective. He'd taken the risk of turning up. He failed to find a nice place to go. He tried to make it special by conjuring a drink she hadn't heard of. He needed her to help him find the words for what this was all about. Why did she say so little? Was she bored? He'd decided to cut things short and let her go home. Though they bumped into each other now and then, nothing more passed between them.

She hasn't thought of him for years but when she is about to search for Raif, it is the engineer who rises up to divert her. He was someone who once came to seek her out and now she wants to know what's happened to him. Is he happy, successful, married, alive, straight or gay, handsome or gone to seed? She could probably find clues to any of this but not to the question of why he came to her room that night and why the lovage mattered.

His name is not unusual and there are dozens of him. One picture shocks her with its familiarity but it's of a boy who is eighteen now and who lives on the other side of the world. The engineer might be this software designer or that butcher, the lawyer, the rugby player or the illustrator. Some have a trace of his sweet features. They smile at her from corporate websites, obituaries, class photos and snaps from a night out. They gather on her screen, variations on someone she barely knew but who once took it upon himself to turn up at her door.

All she is to Raif is whatever she reminds him of. She tells herself this and it makes her feel wise. But if Iris were to reach out to him, as if opening a door, the atmosphere would grow dense with past detail. There'd be a drag on her action as if the air had become too thick to move through. Such a gesture would look effortful, too deliberate and invested – which is exactly what it would be.

anywhere

When you start to move through the world beside someone, you might say that you think about them all the time. Mostly you're thinking about how you feel and their idea of you and the possibilities this brings.

When Raif met Liis she'd been sent to London from Milwaukee to teach office managers about the computer systems her company sold. She would be there for three months and then they'd move her on. To Germany, she thought, or perhaps Australia, she wasn't sure.

She lived in a company flat in a mansion block close to the centre of the city. It had neither character nor detail but a solidity that Raif, who grew up in a house that was still being built, found amazing. He relished the heft of the glossy dark doors, how the carpet in the foyer pushed back against his shoes, and the lift in which they had to stand so thrillingly close that he made a game of it, refusing to touch her. The lift climbed so gradually that it seemed to collude in this tension and the corridor leading to her flat was narrow enough to sustain it. They still did not touch. But as soon as the front door was closed, Liis pulled him towards her and he found his way inside her as quickly as he could. They fucked on every one of that flat's neutral surfaces: on the putty-coloured carpet, the cardboard-brown leatherette sofa, on the fake-marble kitchen counter, up against the pale-mushroom walls. They rarely fucked in the bed.

The flat had no pictures or ornaments. Everything in it worked perfectly, every drawer closed silently and the doors shut completely. Raif saw the entire block as a smooth machine full of smooth machines like Liis. He was incomplete and inept. He hesitated and wondered. He did not belong in such a world and so he craved it.

They often woke in the small hours at the same moment and talked in the dark. These were their deepest conversations and were neither continued nor referred to again.

You're not really English, are you? she asked without embarrassment.

People usually found a more oblique way to approach the subject, asking too soon where he grew up.

My father was from Mauritius. His mother was Japanese.

But your name is Arabic?

It was my grandfather's name. He was from another island.

Show me.

She produced an atlas and showed him a page that was mostly sea. She waited for him to point at where he came from but he wasn't quite sure. To him these were stories, not places. Liis traced a line from west to east, from one tiny island to another.

And your mother? she asked.

English, I suppose. But mostly Irish. My parents were both Catholics, which made it a bit easier.

A Catholic only child?

My mother says that she couldn't wait to get back to work – she's a radiographer.

He was learning that Liis liked to make sense of things

but did not pursue the matter of feelings.

So you come from four islands.

I don't think of myself as coming from anywhere.

Everyone on an island arrived there from somewhere else.

This delighted Raif. At school he had been called *different* and the harder the other children found it to place him, the fiercer the question became: *Who are you?* They couldn't make sense of his face and neither could he. When he looked in the mirror he asked the same question – not *Who am I?* but *Who are you?*

The slight child who looked a bit foreign had been transformed, over the course of one summer, into a young man whose face drew everyone's gaze. Girls appeared wherever he was and switched themselves on. He was surrounded by smiling girls, laughing girls, girls who puffed their hair, laid a hand on his arm and leant towards him in their straining shirts, who offered him the right to their attention and perhaps to their bodies. The other boys thought this hilarious and then annoying.

They were on their way out of the world of school, and the king of the boys knew that this year was to be the last of his reign so he made good use of what power he had. When the queen of the girls started to pay attention to Raif, the king of the boys shoved him against a wall, chanting the old question: *Who are you?* Only now it was a demand that Raif give up becoming this bright new self. He complied and sank back. The queen of the girls walked past as if she'd never met him and the king of the boys did so too.

This taught Raif that to have someone's attention is a

dangerous thing. He looked away for years and when he looked again, he saw Liis. She arrived in his life and he became the man from four islands whose face people kept returning to, unable to complete their reading. The question was still the same – *Who are you?* – but he was learning that it didn't require an answer and that not offering one was a kind of power.

When Raif remarked that Liis's life seemed to have been a series of epic histories, she laughed and said she grew up very quietly in a village cut off from the sea by a military zone she was not permitted to enter. She was disliked at school because her father worked for the government.

I don't need to belong, she said. It doesn't mean anything.

It felt to Raif as if she were cutting him free, which made him want to be bound to her forever.

I wanted to belong, he said, and then I didn't and now I do.

You want to?

No, I do belong. With you.

Liis accepted this as if it were not terribly important. For Raif it was the greatest possible expression of happiness.

They married when her visa expired. She said she didn't want to continue in her job or return to the States and he was proud of being able to offer himself as a solution. He started his first teaching post and they rented the flat he still lives in at the end of a new extension to an underground line. Their life took on the structures and rhythms Liis gave it and he was glad to conform. She decorated their home in the smart, neutral tones of the company flat, only now the putty and mushroom decor was not to be disturbed. If they had sex at all it was in bed.

Liis signed up with an elite temp agency and went to a different office every few months, adjusting to complex new systems and procedures each time. She would make observations about the people she met but she was never drawn in. She walked out of whatever office she was in that day as if she were never going there again and arrived home empty-handed. She asked Raif about his research, made logical encouraging remarks and cooked beautiful food that tasted of nothing.

I've made some delicious chicken, she would say. Another pancake? They're delicious.

He would eat some more and agree that they really were delicious.

Within a few years he'd written his book about absence in the seventeenth-century curiosity cabinet. It was twice as long as had been planned and, for a work full of extraordinary objects, strikingly dull. Raif had watched himself move his research into place. He couldn't think of anything to add.

He blamed whatever strain he felt on the book and Liis encouraged this.

He had pains in his stomach after each beautiful meal.

Female warmth – from colleagues and friends – was overwhelming. He distanced himself by imagining the details of their bodies.

He masturbated at work and cried often at his desk.

When Liis began to complain of headaches, he accepted this as another stage in her withdrawal. It took him a long time to understand that she was ill. It was pain that broke her open in the end but then she spoke her own language, which he did not understand.

He thought only about her and not about himself and believed this to be love. Only much later did he wonder at her nature and later still, his own.

is he flirting with her?

Iris does not see Raif as a man slipping on ice, whose friends are bored with the inertia of his grief and whose mind fixes on smaller and smaller detail. She knows he is an academic, that his father is dead and that he has a colleague who slips her arm through his. Otherwise he is in outline.

For him, Iris is an atmosphere. He can't see her but what she suggests is palpable. He tells himself that he has found a colleague who shares his interests, and he prints off an image of the cloud mirror she mentioned, which he immediately loses among the papers on his desk. Now and then it surfaces and he looks at it and loses it again until the day he throws it in the bin and decides to get in touch.

Raif's message says that he'd like to know more about some of the objects Iris mentioned: the cloud mirror, the merman, the jealousy glass, the bone skates. Perhaps she could give him references and catalogue numbers. *My subject is more broadly curiosity*, he writes. Is he flirting with her? Iris knows that she could send him these details or invite him to see the objects. He's forcing her to be the one who suggests they meet. In a small room in her head she sees them years later and he's saying *You asked me to come to see you. You started it.* (Started what?)

She sends him a list of references, links and catalogue numbers, and tells him who to contact if he wants to view anything. She adds her best wishes. A month passes and Iris starts to feel as if she's waiting for an echo. One day she comes across an image of the merman and is about to send it to him but this is supposed to be a casual contact and the merman is not a casual thing. She finds a photo of the cloud mirror and sends that instead – as if the cloud mirror has nothing to suggest.

the cloud mirror

The 1862 International Exhibition covered twenty acres of the site on which the street of museums now stands. Great halls of cast iron, brick and glass were filled with cotton mills and ship's engines, submarine cables, electronic telegraph machines, sculpture and wallpaper. Among all this, James Goddard demonstrated two small instruments. One was a device for measuring sunlight hours through the use of photographic paper and the other was the cloud mirror. A mahogany disc the size of a dinner plate, it contained a small mirror surrounded by a paper collar on which the cardinal points had been broken down into south, south-west, south-south-west and so on. The idea was that it could be used to track the speed and direction of clouds and so better predict the weather.

That same year a scientist called James Glaisher decided to find out more about clouds by going up among them. The only way to do this was in a hot-air balloon. He had a willing companion in Henry Coxwell, a dentist with a lifelong passion for ballooning, and together they designed a balloon that was eighty feet tall. They chose a site in Wolverhampton, as inland as they could possibly get. Glaisher brought along seventeen instruments with which to monitor the air.

They rose easily to five thousand feet. *On emerging from the cloud at seventeen minutes past one, we came into a flood of light, with a beautiful blue sky without a cloud above us, and a magnificent sea of cloud below . . . I tried to take a view of their surface with the camera, but the balloon was ascending too rapidly and spiralling too quickly to allow me to do so.*

They were now in a perfect position in relation to their subject. If only they could then have remained there! The balloon continued to climb. *The height of two miles was reached at twenty-one minutes past one.* The temperature had dropped to freezing. They jettisoned sand but still the balloon rose. Eventually they were at an altitude of around five miles. A line became tangled and the dentist clambered up to free it. After that he found it difficult to catch his breath. Glaisher continued to monitor his instruments but was now having trouble making sense of them: *I could not see the fine column of the mercury in the wet-bulb thermometer; nor the hands of the watch, nor the fine divisions on any instrument.* He started to lose sensation and then found himself unable to move and passed out. Coxwell had somehow to release the valve and start bringing the balloon back down but his hands had lost all feeling and were turning black.

They continued to float upwards into thinner air, the dentist watching the balloon expand, knowing that eventually it would burst. He pulled himself by the elbows up onto the rigging and managed to tug at the rip-cord with his teeth. At last the balloon began to descend. The pressure dropped and the scientist revived (having been unconscious for seven minutes). He checked his instruments and poured brandy on Coxwell's numb hands.

No inconvenience followed our insensibility.

They made it safely back down to earth but what had they learnt, these Victorian boffins in their autumn tweeds? They learnt only what had happened to them while understanding very little about it.

How else do we begin in the knowledge of something? They went on to make more flights and Glaisher, by returning to his subject and persisting in his measurements and records, made vital contributions to our understanding of rain formation and wind speed.

Neither Raif nor Iris would have gone up in that balloon. He would have sought out contemporary newspaper reports of the experiment and records of the economic impact of unpredictable weather. She would have analysed the balloon's materials, construction and durability. In this they were more like the inventor of the cloud mirror – preferring to observe rather than to enter their subject, and to look down rather than up.

meeting point

The image of the cloud mirror that Iris sends to Raif is the same one he printed for himself. Still he prints it again. He ought to go to see it. He tells his students that they mustn't rely on images any more than they should secondary sources. Where possible, they must see the thing itself. So he writes to Iris and says he's coming to look up something in the museum's library and wonders if she could show him the cloud mirror.

Now he's standing next to her in a research room at the museum. The lighting is thorough and both feel exposed. The summer has got stuck, as it always does, in a series of grey days. The city is unbreathable and its people feel guarded and ashamed. They will submit to the crowd but encounters such as this, when the body comes under the scrutiny of someone known, are to be avoided. Raif is conscious of a pooling under his arms. Iris is suddenly aware of the slick wet of the nape of her neck, the river at her lower back. They keep turning away as if it is the other who is bringing about this terrible liquefaction.

She struggles to put on gloves, offers him a pair, unpacks the cloud mirror and passes it over. He hadn't expected the real thing to be quite so ordinary. Iris explains that the frame was coated with an unstable varnish she wants to assess but she's not sure how to treat the wood without damaging the brittle paper collar. He asks how she'll decide this and she explains that she's been trained to identify the most fragile component of any object and to make protecting that her priority. She's probably going to recommend that the varnish is left untouched.

She's impressed by the time he's taking to study the cloud mirror and looks forward to what he might say. Eventually he puts it down.

So a cloud could be said to be travelling in any one of thirty-two directions.

Really? (She knows this.)

He picks it up again and looks at her with a big smile he's borrowed from somewhere.

Shall we give it a whirl?

He takes it towards the room's one small window, which is usually closed but has been left open as the day is so close. Iris is alarmed.

You can't—

Raif, caught up in his performance of daring, is slow to gauge her tone.

You mean you've never tried to see how it works?

Iris is baffled. Does he not know how to handle such things?

It shouldn't be exposed. The ink, the paper . . .

Of course, he says. Stupid of me.

As she takes the cloud mirror from him she sees a spasm pass across his face which she decides is annoyance, anger even. She's right that he's furious but only with himself. He's always done his best to be correct and was trying to impress her by being less so. She busies herself packing the mirror away.

You can tell that it wouldn't work all that well, she says. It was just a prototype and didn't get taken up.

It might have been useful in the field – to farmers and military strategists.

Do you think so?

No, not really.

Iris has gone to some trouble to retrieve the cloud mirror. It's her gift to him and now that he's disappointed so is she. He's smaller than she remembers, thickening at the waist and even a little womanly about the hips. His hair is ominously fine but his looks don't depend on it. She notes these details as a way of calming herself down because her body has switched itself on, as it did when they first met. She is so aware of the warmth and scent of his skin that she might as well be touching him, they might as well be pressed together, inside one another, right here.

He thanks her and picks up his jacket. So he has seen the cloud mirror. What else? He'd said in his message that he was coming to the library and now he recalls a footnote to a chapter that he's been meaning to pursue.

I'll walk you out, Iris says. The quickest way is down the back stairs and through the central hall but if you're interested, and have time, I could show you the new gallery?

Raif confuses his desire to escape this room with a desire to escape her.

No. That's kind of you but I have to . . . The library closes in an hour.

The library. Of course.

Another time.

No need.

Now that he's mentioned the library, he must go there. He orders a book and looks at it.

At half past five Raif makes his way to the underground. He's late for a supervision with a doctoral student but doesn't rush. A train is waiting at the platform and he stands before it. He remembers having to stand close to Iris, closer than he would have chosen. He doesn't move.

Fuck! someone erupts from a cluster of people hurrying cautiously down the stairs onto the platform, hoping to catch this train. *Fuck!* the boy yells again as he loses his balance and stumbles, knocking someone over. He's young and gathers himself without hesitation, bouncing back up and onto the train just as the doors close.

The woman the boy knocked over is sitting on a step gathering up the things that have spilt from her bag. It's Iris. There are people muttering sympathy and indignation and asking her if she's alright and she's nodding her head without looking up because for some absurd reason – she wasn't hurt, not even all that surprised – she's trying not to cry.

Raif approaches, leans down to help pick up her things and finds himself offering her a tampon, an empty blister pack of painkillers and her phone. Not knowing what to do next, he takes her hand and raises her to her feet and they pause in the moment as they did on first meeting when passing through that doorway side by side. Having helped her up and brushed the dirt off the sleeve of her jacket, he doesn't touch her again, although he asks three times if she's sure she's alright.

To those around them it seems as if these two people, colleagues surely, are passing the time on their way home. Who can tell that they've right now reached the purest stage of connection? Thanks to the minor accident that has just occurred, they're gathering substance. This is the first thing to have *happened* to them.

Their affinity has yet to be tested or applied and so is easy to believe in. They know almost nothing about one another but if one had to describe the other, they would do so confidently and in the most idealised terms. If one said they were about to travel the world and would be gone for six months, the other would wish them well. They would feel neither left nor that they were leaving someone because they are not yet part of each other's lives.

A train pulls in and Iris suddenly says that she's forgotten something and must go back to her office and that it was nice to see him and she hopes his visit has been helpful. He watches her struggle back up the stairs through the next wave of passengers, who then surround him. When the train moves off he's still there on the briefly empty platform. If only she were there too. If they could stay where they are, before any sort of map is drawn, their relationship would be perfect.

varnish

Iris met David on the underground. It was late in the evening and there were only a handful of people in the carriage. She was sitting opposite and along from him, lost inside a stiff white dress she'd made herself. Her face was emphatic and her hair was cut as if it were just something to get out of the way. She held an open book in her hands but kept her eyes fixed on the window opposite. He couldn't get a sense of the body beneath her dress and enjoyed speculating on this. She wasn't delicate and he liked that. Her limbs were heavy and shapely, her hands blunt.

The train slowed as it neared her station but just as she moved towards the door, it stopped. Underground trains stop all the time and for the first thirty seconds most people pay little attention. Thirty seconds is a pause. Longer than that and it becomes a delay and the passengers, who have been dreaming, reading and sleeping, become present. It's as if they wake up, each saying *I am here, in this small space, with strangers, inside the earth, and I cannot move*. After two minutes the possibility of moving seems far less likely than that of being stuck there for hours.

David noticed that she kept looking from door to window. Eventually she sat down again and got out her book. Her eyes were shut, her hands shaking. He went over and sat beside her.

Were you looking for something?

She surprised herself by answering him honestly but kept her eyes shut.

I'm wondering how to escape, if we need to.

You can always escape.

How?

The doors can be opened, the windows can be smashed. There's a hammer for that exact purpose in a box over there.

But we're not going to do that so for now we're stuck.

We're not even really underground. Just tucked inside a tunnel. The driver can probably see the platform.

David didn't ask what she feared might happen.

I like your dress, he said and then shrugged.

As Iris turned towards him, the train started to move. David pretended that it was his stop too and followed her out of the station. She hurried ahead.

I was on my way east, he called after her. Only I liked your dress.

She walked back and gave him her card. She'd printed them herself and he was the first person she'd given one to. It announced her as Conservator of Inlaid Objects.

They started as rescuer and rescued. He was drawn to her concentration and she to a source of relief. He never asked why she'd felt so panicked. People do ask these things, as if there are clear reasons. We come up with answers and these become our reasons.

David arrived the next morning at the address on the card. It was a solid suburban villa with a subdued privet hedge and a paved front garden. When Iris came to the door she too looked less remarkable than he expected. She led him upstairs to a tightly organised bedsit and explained that the house had belonged to a couple who collected inlaid objects. The downstairs rooms had been filled with their acquisitions and they'd retreated to live upstairs. The couple's son had inherited the house and packed up the collection. He then decided that he wanted it all restored and valued before offering it for sale. Iris was a friend of his daughter's. He was impressed that she had a PhD and didn't want to waste money on a proper expert (he'd phoned one or two) or time carting this stuff about.

There were ash and ebony trays, pewter and mother-of-pearl boxes, screens inlaid with tortoiseshell, a walnut clothes brush inlaid with silver, a comb of boxwood and ivory, a tortoiseshell snuff box and Roman buttons of mosaic butterflies inlaid on porphyry. One or two things were museum standard but many appeared, when Iris scrutinised them more carefully, to be fakes.

The son was furious. He'd grown up with objects more cherished than he had been himself and understood them to be of extraordinary worth. His parents were experts. They'd scoured auctions and catalogues and were friends with the best dealers.

My parents did not buy fakes.

If you could locate the bills of sale, we might be able to verify their origins.

The dealers they bought them from were friends. There wasn't much paperwork.

The son turned towards the largest object in the collection, a Chinese screen.

Look, love. I know you're fresh out of college and don't yet have an eye but this is tortoiseshell.

It's actually a form of plastic. It's very well done but the discoloration is an unarguable sign.

It's old.

It's fake.

Iris was young. She thought he'd be glad of the truth. When she'd confirmed that it was plastic, she'd been thrilled. Why shouldn't he be thrilled too?

It's tortoiseshell, the son said. It says so here in my parents' catalogue. They were experts. They would have known.

Iris realised that it was her job to give him the information he wanted. They were his objects. And now that she'd raised doubts about their authenticity, he'd be forced either to sell them as fakes or knowingly pass them off as genuine. No wonder he was angry. She tried to think of something conciliatory to say.

Even real tortoiseshell isn't real. It's usually turtle.

These are not fakes.

Fakes are a legitimate part of cultural history, she explained. They are an art in themselves.

Fakes have no value.

Museums are full of them.

The son was in his sixties and lived three hundred miles away. He did not have the patience for this. He told Iris to identify the most valuable objects, to clean them and write up an inventory. The next time he came down, she'd laid them out.

They look a bit dingy, he said.

I could give the wood a coat of varnish, she said.

She did what she'd been taught to do: to protect something by sealing its surfaces. She didn't know that twenty years later she'd be removing this kind of varnish wherever she could. She would also learn to ask if restoring an object would expose it to more harm. If an eighteenth-century marquetry tea caddy was varnished forty years ago, should that varnish be removed as inauthentic? Or was it now part of the object's story? And what did it mean to restore something when you could never make it new?

David wore clothes which adapted to any occasion, in colours Iris couldn't name. It was important to her that he wore them carelessly and he was still young enough, at thirty, for this to look boyish rather than sad. Her idea of him continued to shift according to her mood. His looks wavered most. For some time she wasn't sure if he was tall or slight, animated or animal. Then he became familiar and she didn't think about what he looked like at all.

David offered her conspiracy. He flattered her with his assumption that she understood his rapid, allusive banter. He mocked and demolished those she held in awe – the director of a museum, the architect of a new gallery extension – and dismissed the most eminent names in her world, whom he appeared to know well. He held out what he could glean, a polished opinion or sharpened snippet of gossip, rather than himself. Iris didn't notice this because she was more comfortable with what he brought than who he might be.

So you design exhibitions? she asked.

In a way.

In what way?

Iris didn't mean this as a challenge. It was characteristic of her to be thorough.

I extrapolate. I interpret. I convey.

He was laughing as he made this pronouncement so she laughed too. He then quizzed her for an hour and she told him about her cautious adolescence in a northern seaside town, her tidy room, how she liked to wear several layers of clothing and that getting drunk felt like adding even more.

He observed the way she sat up straight and built her sentences and when she'd finished he proclaimed her:

Iris the iridescent, the refracted, the divine! Conceived on the darkest coldest edge of the North Sea under great cliffs in a place of iron and slate! Iris of the purest colours, glimpsed only in a rainbow or in oil on water! Iris the precise, Iris of the strata, Iris who needs specific atmospheric conditions in order to reveal herself!

His vision of this strong-limbed woman in a white dress was already varnished. Her desire to escape from the carriage of an underground train brightened into noble ambition, her fear a supreme acuity. When he met her for the second time, she seemed quite relaxed. Would she ever need rescuing again?

After the moment of yes and the decision to follow someone comes the matter of time and place. David waited a long time to sleep with Iris. This wasn't difficult because it was in keeping with his idea of her. He was in love with Iris and desired her above anyone else but sex was at times an abrupt and separate matter. He had one or two special friends and he experienced neither guilt nor power in this.

One night they lay down and Iris asked him what he wanted her to do.

Undress me, he said.

She undid the buttons on his sludge-lemon shirt. She kissed his narrow chest, which was robust and not (as she'd imagined) bird-like at all. He lay back, imperfect, aroused and open to scrutiny. She felt for the second time that he was showing her the way out of a place where she'd got stuck, and she stood up and undressed too.

She meant to do this quickly, just get out of her clothes and lie down beside him, but when David glimpsed her strong round breasts he gave such a desirous sigh that Iris felt proud and stood back, adjusting to this unexpected pleasure: someone who allowed her effect but did not encroach. She sat in the armchair and parted her legs, just a little at first and then wide.

For the first year of Iris and David's life together, the most loving moments occurred in such rooms. They discovered together how exciting it is to see and be seen by someone who keeps meeting you in the act. Sex became focused on the space between them and how long they could sustain it. David might ask Iris to turn her back so that he could trace, with his eyes, her long waist and broad hips.

Your parts are so defined, he said.

They were twenty-eight and thirty. Their natures were more fixed than they knew but they didn't feel the drag of pattern or memory on each fresh encounter yet. Later he would declare her mechanical but for now he found her body powerful, and pliable too. They lay in the dark and he surrounded her, his fingers in her mouth, his penis deep inside her, his tongue on her breast. She was thrilled by his body's changeable nature, how it could be fluid or rigid, resistant or generous. She would rename him inconsistent, unstable and deceitful soon enough.

David had unlocked the stranger he'd found. He didn't wonder what she contained or why she'd been locked in the first place. They looked and looked at each other but not deeply within. He didn't detect the trauma at her core. She thought he'd seen it and had known not to disturb it. She gave herself to someone she believed had looked beneath the surface and seen the worst of her and had not turned away.

withdrawn memory

The city with its millions is a place where we think we drift and so we greet any chance meetings with exclamations of disbelief. *What are you doing here?* we ask one another and feel obliged to provide an answer. No one drifts.

Still the city persuades us that the first meeting with a lover is a matter of chance. When you are one among millions, there's always a sense that had your lover turned right instead of left, looked up instead of down, she or he would be getting caught up with someone else.

Those who like to get caught up must be prepared to get lost. Perhaps they don't cherish their own substance or maybe they're so sure of themselves that they can dissolve into the city confident that they will emerge again.

When we're young we assume that we'll wake up from any adventure back at home in our own solid beds, as our familiar selves, and mostly we do. But we all have dreams from which we have not entirely woken. No wonder the girl in her party dress out cold on the train or the boy crouched in the doorway with his head buried in his knees bring us such pain. In them we see our lost dreaming selves and we cannot bear them.

Iris grew up having bad dreams. This is how her parents and doctors referred to them but they were not dreams. At any time of day she could experience a lapse in reality. She found herself in an abstract space about to see a terrible thing. All she could do was try to stop time so that the thing didn't appear. Her parents thought she was having seizures but the doctors said there was nothing wrong and sent her, aged ten, to a psychotherapist.

What do you see?

Nothing.

What are you frightened of?

The nothing.

What does the nothing look like?

It looks like nothing.

The therapist tried another approach, asking Iris if she knew someone who'd seen a terrible thing.

My gran.

Did she tell you about it?

My mum told me the story but it's not a story. It happened.

What happened?

My gran was in a place and she saw a terrible thing and that's why I must never ask her.

But your mum told you what happened.

I told you what happened. Gran was in a place and she saw a thing.

How did your mum describe this place and this thing?

I don't know. I can't remember.

Would you like to ask her?

Iris did not want to ask her grandmother what she had seen because then she would see it too. She didn't know how to say this so she told the therapist as much as she could of what her mother had told her. *Your grandmother is quiet because something happened to her. She saw a terrible thing.* When she thought about it, Iris couldn't even be sure her mother had said that. She couldn't remember not knowing this story or when she had been told. She just knew it and she knew that when she had the bad dream she was in the same place as her grandmother. She also knew (without being able to say how) that this story was one that neither her mother nor her grandmother could bear. That Iris must bear it for them.

As she got older these lapses became so rare that eventually they passed from memory into dream. They were neither referred to nor discussed and Iris persuaded herself that she'd invented the whole thing – not only *the nothing* but what her mother had said.

We can inherit bad dreams just as we might a gesture. We have our great-aunt's way of biting her lip or raising her arms when she's annoyed, even though she died before we were born. We repeat things we've never known.

curiosity

Are we our worst pain? Raif types the words and stops. He's trying to write a proposal for a conference about curiosity, anomaly and the body. It's years since he's done anything like this. He'd been getting bored, or was it tired, and then his wife died and no one pressed him to do anything. He's lost track of what matters. Current thinking seems to be about how to approach the study of objects. There's not so much about the objects themselves. Or is there? He hasn't kept up.

He distracts himself by clicking through the site of the museum where Iris works. He wanders the collections and selects an object at random. It's a small bronze figure of a woman with a large goitre – nineteenth-century, found in Nigeria and thought to be either an amulet or a teaching aid. He tells himself to think. Her pain would have defined her voice, if she had one. People might have listened to her more carefully. Perhaps she was venerated for this great swelling in her throat?

Curiosity has been Raif's starting point for twenty years. He intends to find out more about the bronze but instead puts Iris's name into the site's search box and works his way through what appears, which is mostly committee notes and acquisition reports. He finds a video of her standing in a room full of shelves of boxes. Her voice is flat and a little harsh and she does not smile. He searches for her name more broadly but nothing much turns up and he's starting to feel uncomfortable. He's been seeing Helen for almost a year and has never been curious enough to search for her.

Rosa knocks on his door.

Are you going to come and have a drink? I'm off tomorrow.

I don't think I can. I'm too—

Sad. I know.

It's not that, I'm just—

See you in six months.

Rosa is off on a research trip. She has no time for Raif and his sadness now. But she notices something.

More offerings?

On a shelf above his desk there's a glass fish, a string of five amber beads, a tiny kaleidoscope, a rose quartz, a disc of silvered mirror, a death-watch beetle, a bird's skull. Rosa goes over to them.

Are they from the same student?

No, it's all sorts.

He gives his lecture on the curiosity cabinet, and the shells and skulls arrive. Perhaps his students can detect how little curiosity he now has and try to provoke it in him.

What am I supposed to do? he says. I can't just throw them away.

Rosa shrugs, says goodbye and goes to meet her friends. She tells them about how the students keep giving Raif these little offerings.

It could be a minefield, someone says.

He's in no danger, says Rosa. He's still mourning his wife.

What about his girlfriend? someone asks. I bumped into them the other day. She looked nice. Tall, pretty, sweet . . .

Rosa has been speaking about him with authority. She and Raif work next door to each other and they talk. He has told her his most private stories: about going to see his father's body and how he came to doubt Liis's version of events. She knows the details of Liis's illness and death, and she sat with him while he cried. He has never mentioned a girlfriend.

I am not what I am

When people ask Helen and Raif how they met, they hesitate because it was online. Helen is happy to say so but Raif has made clear that he is not. His profile was set up by his cousins, girls in their twenties. They are triplets, born by IVF to Raif's aunt Sorcha when she was forty, and named Jessica, Ashley and Emily because their parents could not decide what to call them and ended up taking the three most popular girls' names of that year from a newspaper.

Raif had been a teenager when the triplets were born but their presence in his life gave him joy. They were tiny creatures with frizzy orange hair who grew up to be noisy, indulged and quick, determined to solve any problem and happy to say everything out loud. They were told from early on that their cousin Raif was *a bit sad*. He'd lost his father and found it hard it fit in. They knew he loved their silliness and exuberance and so this was what they continued to offer him.

When Liis died they turned up at the flat, put on music and poured gin. They told him on the spot that he would be allowed a year to grieve and then they would find him someone and they had. There was a photo of a kind and pretty face, and a quote.

> I am not merry; but I do beguile
> The thing I am, by seeming otherwise.

Raif copied it into a search engine and found that it was a speech of Desdemona's from *Othello*. He found another quote from the play and sent it to Helen.

> But I will wear my heart upon my sleeve
> For daws to peck at: I am not what I am.

Helen was touched and impressed. She said so when they met.

It must have been exactly how you felt when creating your profile.

He didn't tell her that he'd had nothing to do with it.

And you? He asked. Why Desdemona?

I played her once. I was only the understudy but I did go on. More than once.

Raif was still thinking about the quote.

Those lines. They say that if you pretend to be happy, you'll become so. Is that your philosophy?

My philosophy? I don't know. Maybe. I chose the quote because it's a puzzle that solves itself.

That's what you aspire to be? A puzzle that solves itself? Why not?

He wondered if he was putting her under strain.

I'm sorry. I can't help thinking—

Thinking what?

Helen was thirty-five. She'd had a long-running role in a radio sitcom but her part was eventually cut. In the meantime she'd lost her footing, such as it was, in television costume drama. She'd played a series of inert young women, usually the confidante or the cousin who lacked grasp. After some difficult years she was now finding out who else she could be.

She liked Raif's face but he wasn't as tall as she'd imagined, and seemed bookish and a bit contrived. Her mind drifted and when he mentioned his wife she didn't catch the context.

Sorry, your wife?

Yes.

You have a wife?

That's what I meant by late – my late wife. She died.

Helen could not understand how she'd missed this.

I'm so sorry. I thought you said—

That she was late?

He smiled, pleased with his quickness, and then realised that he'd just made a joke about his dead wife.

My wife died a year ago. And I—

Has there been anyone since?

She said it so gently that Raif did not detect any urgency. All the same, he lied.

No one.

That first winter had been a desperate period and he had drawn a line and was now himself again.

Any first meeting brings with it a chance of renewal. As Raif and Helen talked, they were selecting, reshaping, rejecting and arranging elements of themselves and their stories. They appeared thoughtful and felt refreshed. Helen guarded her reactions to the extent that Raif thought her incredibly relaxed. Talking to her was like being smoothed out and his perception of her softened. Perhaps she wasn't taller than him after all. He wanted to stroke the bouncy hair that he'd at first judged too girlish, and as she leant towards him he had to pull his gaze away from the deep neckline of her petalled dress.

Like Raif, Helen was revising her first impressions. The death of his wife obliterated minor detail and now she saw him more simply. He was serious and attractive.

What was it like? she asked. Afterwards. What did you do? The next day?

I suppose I carried on. Doing the usual things.

You must have been beside yourself.

He'd watched himself navigate each day, each conversation. Beside himself? Perhaps so.

Helen considered the situation. He'd had a year to grieve and do stupid things and now he would be ready. She was not as calculating as this sounds. So many of the men she'd met online had been just out of, or on their way out of, a marriage. They were always keen to see her a second time but after a few weeks either disappeared or provoked an ending.

You're just too nice, a paramedic she'd met the year before had said as he slopped beer down the front of her dress in the crowded pub where he'd insisted they meet.

Sorry, what? She couldn't hear him.

Nice! he shouted just as the noise level dropped. I'm sorry, love, but you're just too nice!

Every man in the place had turned to evaluate her and she can still see them nodding their agreement. *Yup. Too nice.*

71

Not wanting to be called nice ever again, Helen equipped herself to perform sex and was pleased with the effect. She read up about techniques and toys and surprised herself by feeling aroused by descriptions of light S&M. The day after meeting Raif she dared herself to go into a boutique-style sex shop where a conspiratorial young man persuaded her to buy something expensive in coral chiffon, and a black wand with an ostrich plume which he demonstrated by stroking the inside of Helen's arm. She had to buy it. One day, not yet, she would let Raif see her in chiffon and silk. She would blindfold him, tie him (lightly) to the bed and run the plume over his body.

The flow of people through the city is itself enough to bring about a loosening of feeling. It's easy to submit, to become a stranger, not far from your own front door. Those who remain in the city believe in change perhaps more than they should.

Raif expected his cousins to be pleased when he reported that he liked Helen and had arranged a second date but they were firmly indifferent. They were staying with him for the weekend, which meant using his flat as a place to get ready for a night on the town. Ashley was a police officer, Emily a psychiatric social worker and Jessica a croupier who also tutored children in maths. When they came into the city, they made the most of it.

The cardboard-coloured sofa was strewn with clothes and books, and the coffee table crammed with nail polish and hair straighteners. Raif didn't mind. The triplets were a concentrated version of everything – three times as much warmth, three times as much life. It suited him to sit in their midst and receive their attention. They interrogated him because they thought it was good for him. He didn't notice how little they revealed of themselves. For all their chatter, they were reserved. They performed being the triplets and then went off to work or alone out to play. Only on these nights when they stayed with Raif did they go out together.

Do you meet people online? he asked them.

Of course we do, all the time.

But what do you call it?

Whatever we want to.

After he'd been on four dates with Helen, they wanted to meet her. Raif wasn't ready for this so instead invited them to come to see her in a play that was just opening called *The Chemist*. It was Helen's first lead role. He didn't think it wise to warn her and he made the triplets sit in a different row. She was playing a chemist whose colleague was in love with her. To stop himself succumbing, he introduced her to his wife, who fell in love with her as well. It was finely written and Helen was at her best. The chemist's intelligence was gloved in a courtly manner and the audience, like the couple, fell under her spell. She pondered nuclei while painting her nails and she always wanted sex.

I think Helen might be just who I'm looking for, Raif announced to the triplets on the way home.

No one responded and so he repeated himself. This time Jessica spoke.

What we mean is she's the first person you've met. What if there's someone else? Someone better? Why not keep looking?

We look for a lover and then we start seeing them. If you are seeing someone, you must not look. In the city there is always someone else.

Raif, feeling more than he had in years, believed that he felt enough. For their fifth date he offered to cook Helen dinner. It was the first time she'd been to his flat. She was surprised by the taupe and cream furnishings. The food – smoked salmon, mushroom risotto – was of similar colours.

Have some risotto, Raif said. It's delicious.

It tasted of nothing but Raif hadn't expected it to. They ate in silence, smiling at one another in an exploratory way. Eventually Raif stood up to clear the plates and then hesitated.

I didn't tell you the truth, he said. I mean about before I met you.

Helen's hand moved to conceal her chest where the chiffon trim, she was suddenly sure of it, could be glimpsed inside the neckline of her dress, and urged him not to say any more. She went to the bathroom, where she discovered that her period had started and the coral knickers were stained with blood. She had no tampons with her and opened the cabinet, surprised to find it crammed with lotions, lipstick, hairspray, scent and an entire shelf of pills stickered with fluorescent warning labels. There was a half-empty box of tampons and Helen gingerly helped herself. Should she tell Raif?

In the kitchen he'd taken three kinds of chocolate pudding out of their packets and arranged them on large plates. He poured on icing sugar and added several stalks of mint.

Those look delicious, said Helen, edging back into her seat as it occurred to her that there might be blood on her dress. It was ridiculous to feel unable to mention it but this man, this flat, the food – everything was so uptight that she was overwhelmed by the fear of making a mess.

Raif had envisaged a dish of tiny and complex delights like the photo in a magazine he'd picked up on a train the week before: chocolate discs, squares and triangles dusted with icing sugar and scattered with mint. The article had been called What She Really Wants and had drawn his eye because he thought it was about sex. It was about chocolate but the idea stuck. The way to get Helen into bed had presented itself. This was the way. Only these puddings were each meant for two people and he'd bought six. They were on offer – buy two packets, get one free – and he'd taken this as an instruction. What She Really Wants.

I seem to have lost my sense of proportion, he said.

Helen laughed so kindly that Raif, too, was overwhelmed. How lovely she was, how understanding! They picked at the puddings before Helen, who'd arrived with the intention of having sex but did not want to negotiate the fact that she was bleeding, said, as encouragingly as possible, that she'd had a lovely evening but was tired and ought to go home. He didn't offer to see her out and she got as far as the corner before a mighty cramp made her double over and vomit chocolate pudding into the gutter. She'd eaten as much as she possibly could.

At home she put her silk knickers to soak in salt water and was glad to be in her own bed. She forgot how uneasy she'd been and just felt sorry for that sad man in his sad flat. How hard he'd tried to impress her! He'd lost his wife (and his sense of proportion) and made food that tasted of nothing. She could help.

Across the city, Raif put the puddings in the bin. Helen had seemed to enjoy herself and then she'd gone home. He accepted the information that she was tired and felt neither sad nor rejected. He took his pill and went online.

Helen had read about grief and she knew that for a time people blunder about, doing things they shouldn't and don't even want to. But they come through it all with new wisdom. So this is what she saw in Raif, who, it is true, had been broken open by Liis's death and for a while had seen life on grand terms. He has no new wisdom although he knows now that the worst thing can happen and that it can render you unable to feel what you feel.

black mist

Iris came to depend on David to make life interesting, just as he needed someone to do this for. He was at his happiest when pulling back the curtain on some dazzling surprise. On the second anniversary of the night they met – a date she had forgotten – he proposed. *I do not love this man enough*, she thought, *but I will not look at that.*

She said yes to David because she was in a life with him already and he did much to enhance that life, leading her into rooms she would ordinarily hesitate to enter. On their wedding night Iris stood, as he asked, before a mirror in their hotel room while he lit six candles and then reverentially undid the buttons that ran down the back of her dress. *I have married a man I do not love enough*, she reminded herself as he slipped the dress from her shoulders and fell on his knees before her. *But perhaps this is as much as I can now love* – as he parted her legs and pressed his face against the lace he'd chosen. She observed the scene in reflection and saw herself as he had named her – refracted and brought to shining life. The image in the mirror became how she remembered her wedding night – as something observed.

As he knelt before her, David already knew that there were layers within this person of layers that he could not disturb. Over the years he stopped thinking of her as colour and light. Iris of the strata would be renamed a creature of stone.

*

Three years after the wedding, Iris came to work for the museum. It was the tail-end of a decade of expansiveness and they could afford to send ten staff to a conference in Baltimore. She'd written a paper on the changing approach of conservators to varnished surfaces and was horrified at the thought of having to present it. But she'd never been to America and was keen to see what it was like to be so far away from home. They stayed in a hotel with many floors and meeting rooms, all upholstered to create a neutral hush. The group from London drew together. They refused name badges, sneered at those who joined in, and stayed up late in the bar. Other travellers joined them, including a man who when asked what he did said that he put out fires.

Actual fires or metaphorical ones? asked a confident blonde curator.

Oil wells. Blowouts, mostly, but also bombed oilfields.

The group fell silent as people thought about what to say and then a loud man sitting next to the blonde, who patted her knee while he talked, came up with:

How does that work? I mean, those fires just burn themselves out, don't they? Nothing to be done.

The fire man didn't bother to counter this and Iris was impressed. She hadn't noticed him sift through the women in the group and come to settle on her.

You were so still, he told her later. And so clear.

Like water, she thought.

At two in the morning there were still a handful of people listening to the fire man talk about the smoke that came from six hundred exploded wells when they burned for seven months and how it sat low in the sky like mile after mile of storm cloud, the black mist and the black rain, and how the land also blackened as sand, soot, ash and oil congealed and set like concrete. People had to use torches in the middle of the day.

The fire man looked at Iris while he spoke. It was becoming their conversation. Eventually everyone stood up and started to say goodnight and when Iris and the fire man stepped into the lift they found themselves alone. Iris pressed the button for her floor. He waited a moment and then, with theatrical delicacy, reached out as if to press a button too but held back and mimed the action instead. Iris thought it the cleverest, most graceful proposition she had ever received.

For years afterwards the fire man arose in her mind as a black mist because as soon as they were alone together she had known nothing of her husband or her life at home. She had stepped into another dimension where the act of fucking this stranger separated itself from what it might mean. She had discovered a capacity in herself which ter- rified and entranced her.

She could not look at what she was doing or, later, at what she had done. She tried but she could not see it. When she got home, David suggested they have a baby. She became pregnant immediately and the black mist cleared.

the little rebellions

When the girls were four and two, David fell off his bike and couldn't get up. He recovered in a matter of hours but was sent for tests. Scans revealed that he had lesions in his brain associated with multiple sclerosis. He might develop the condition and he might not. He continued to work as sporadically as ever for a series of short-lived design companies. He remained his lazy, playful self but his diagnosis brought a new tone to everything. Iris and the children learnt not to comment if he stuttered or stumbled or went to lie down. There were episodes when he lost his balance, his vision blurred or he wet himself, but he always recovered. He called these his body's *little rebellions*.

Iris suspected he made half of them up.

Rebellion against what? she snapped one day. Itself?

And she remembered that of course that was exactly what his body was doing just as he punched the air and said the very word she was thinking.

Exactly.

She had been gathering herself to say that she no longer wanted to live with him but she couldn't think of a good enough reason now. It didn't help that the house was so small. It had been advertised as a railway cottage and they'd been charmed by the idea of a cottage in the city. What it meant was old and cramped. The double bed took up most of their room and the bathroom was a functional jostle. They took out a loan to convert the attic into a room for the girls. Iris kept half her clothes in the cupboard under the stairs. She juggled bills and mortgage payments, saved nothing and shifted debt around. The house became more valuable every day but all she could see were the cracks that ran across every ceiling. Was it enough to say to David that she wanted him to leave because she was so tired?

She lived with him for another six years, going off to bed each night knowing that he would spend the next three hours online. He would tell her in the morning about the things he'd learnt and the deals he'd found. Once she asked him straight out how much porn he watched and he said as much as he wanted when in truth he rarely bothered.

A spell had been cast. David issued warnings while he cooked about how awful the food was going to be and it was. He'd paint a wall in one sketchy coat, pull up flowers instead of weeds, wash the dishes and leave them coated with grease. Iris would ask him to pick up bread and he'd come home with milk. She, too, lost the will to do what was required. She left teacups wherever she put them down and her best dresses on the floor. When she broke things she put them on the kitchen windowsill among the pots of dead herbs as if someone (who?) would come along and mend them.

They got used to having to give the warped front door a shove as they turned the key. They observed damp blossoming in the walls. When they decided they could afford to re-cover the sofa, they chose a fabric neither of them liked.

Now and then something in Iris would rise up and she'd make a romantic gesture, the kind that was obvious and courtly, in the hope that David would meet her in it and their grace would be restored. She'd seen an old tiepin in a jeweller's shop that kept coming to mind. It was a gold bar set with grey topaz, a stormy-looking stone that she loved. When it was placed in her hands, it seemed like something powerful enough to charm her careless husband.

She gave it to him one evening as they were getting into bed.

What's this?

He lifted it out of its box.

A tiepin.

Why would I want a tiepin? I don't wear ties.

It's a beautiful thing that I wanted to give you.

Give me? What for?

He had gone blank, as he did when needing to deflect her. *What is a tiepin? What is beautiful?*

It's grey topaz, she said. And gold.

David put the pin down next to its box and left it there. What was the trap? There had to be one. Every conversation with his wife felt like a trap these days. Why would she buy him something like that? Especially now. The next day Iris put it away in his desk. Neither mentioned it again.

Then David stopped locking doors or closing anything – a cupboard, a drawer, a book. Iris unpacked shopping onto the table and left it there, the empty bags included. She started to open envelopes and then dropped them back on the mat. Her migraines increased. Most Saturdays she left him to cope with the girls while she lay in the dark

82

wondering if she was making her illness up. She felt so much pain that she couldn't tell.

Dropping plates and walking over dresses, she took his unreliability as insult and then as attack. One day she was sitting at the kitchen table with three friends when David came in, said hello, took a beer from the fridge and went to get a glass.

Close the door, Iris said, pointing at the fridge.

David took his time choosing a glass and pouring the beer.

Close the door.

He could have reached back with his hand and done so but now that she had asked, he wouldn't. Iris's friends left soon after.

Who am I to you? she asked him.

I don't know.

Why can't you say something?

I just did.

Not that.

What, then? What is it you want me to say?

I'm not going to hand you a fucking script.

He had sex now and then with women he met through work. They were often young, though this wasn't what attracted him most. He was drawn to a tautness that wasn't just physical: a bouncing energy that made him think of porpoises. These women swam through his fantasies and slipped out of his arms. They thought they were being sophisticated and perhaps they were. They knew they'd never become like his generation with all its wreckage and compromise.

When Iris came to one of David's work events, she sometimes encountered a woman who, it was clear, was either flirting or sleeping with him. Iris, too, thought of porpoises – their fixed faces, elastic responses and urgent repetitions. *Don't pity me*, she wanted to say, but they did. They thought she was sad because her husband didn't desire her any more. They couldn't yet imagine defining happiness any other way.

The last time Iris went to one of these events she had been talking to a man she vaguely knew when she mentioned David and they both looked across the room at him. At that moment, a woman carrying a tray of food made her way past David and, as she did so, rubbed her hip in a confident leisurely way against his body. The fact that he did not react, the complacent expression on the woman's face, told Iris everything.

Don't you find it insulting? the man said.

Sometimes strangers give themselves permission to speak of what they see. As if coming from someone unknown, the words mean nothing. He realised that Iris was shocked, and apologised and hurried away.

At that point the woman with the tray appeared and introduced herself, saying that she worked with David and how lovely it was to meet Iris and that no, she wasn't a professional cook but just did this to help out. It was fun. And Iris smiled and said nothing because she felt nothing and that was what had shocked her.

Their nights were long interrogations of words neither meant about actions neither intended. But there were also truthful exchanges.

Why do you fuck other women? Iris asked once while they were making the bed.

David thought hard before answering.

To bring myself, us, this, back to life.

But it's what's killing us.

Is it.

That was when she had taken off her ring. David had never worn one.

a pattern

David tells people that Iris threw him out but the truth is that she asked him to go to stay at his sister's after their last conversation about Sandra. He and Sandra had grown up together. When she took a job with an arts foundation in the city, their paths started to cross. Iris had met her a few times and thought there was something compensatory in how attentive she'd been. *What do you need?* Iris wanted to ask. What did Iris need? Not to know. Until, quite suddenly, she did.

David kept his phone in his pocket and beside him at night. Iris had the strong feeling that if she looked she would find something and so she didn't. She tried to concentrate on their life as a happy one and in many ways it was. They were often a happy family. Iris and David still had interesting things to tell one another and they went on having good sex. Her body kept telling her things but she'd got used to the pain and set whatever she noticed aside until one day she couldn't.

Did anything happen between you and Sandra?

David's answer swerved across her question.

I've known her forever.

I don't mean now, I mean—

She's got a four-year-old son.

I know that. That's not what I'm talking about. I just wondered—

The father is involved, you know.

I didn't ask about the father.

Iris retreated but she waited. Sandra employed David from time to time as an advisor or tutor, and just when he was about to set up a seminar programme for her, he came home and said that he would no longer be working for the foundation.

Have you fallen out with Sandra?

We can't work together. She's mad.

But something must have happened.

Alright. It did. She wanted us to have an affair.

And what did you say?

She's mad.

That's what you said?

Of course not. I said of course not – because I'm married to you, aren't I? I don't know. She got really angry and so we can't, can we?

Work together or have an affair?

Iris was seeing things she hadn't before because now they made a pattern. David's elaborate justification for some disappearance or delay. Calling her in the afternoon when he was away to pre-empt her calling at night. The condoms that turned up years after they stopped using them. And then there was how David had spoken of Sandra. He'd called her mad. There were other women, ones Iris had wondered about, that David had called mad. Did this mean he'd slept with them too? Who is he? Iris wondered more and more. *Who are you?*

She was seeing anything in anything. The way he hesitated before answering basic questions. *Which train?*

Where did you eat? Why it took him so long to buy bread. Why he was late or forgot or looked past her. Was she mad too?

Her anger became so deep that she could only risk letting it out in small bursts of temper. The last time they did anything together as a family had been on Iris's birthday. David said he'd book her favourite restaurant but when they arrived, it turned out he hadn't. They waited thirty minutes for a table. Iris silenced herself until the end of the meal when the bill came and David passed it to her and then took it back saying that it was a joke. When the waiter left, she began.

It wasn't a fucking joke.

She saw the girls flinch but knew she would let herself continue.

And you didn't forget to book a table. You couldn't be bothered.

Lou grabbed Kate's hand. David pushed his chair back and threw out his arms in a giant shrug. Iris was gripping the table so as not to slap his face.

It was too much to ask, wasn't it? Even though you offered, you couldn't bring yourself to—

Stop it! yelled Lou. Just stop it!

It took Iris a moment to realise that Lou meant her.

At Christmas they'd gone to David's parents as usual. Kate and Lou came to life and disappeared off with their cousins. David lay down on a bench in the kitchen. Later he would lie on the sofa or the floor. This had nothing to do with his illness. He had come home and was fifteen again and needed to lie down. David's parents were particularly kind to Iris, which made her want to lie down too.

David was the son of a couple who adored each other and who liked their children to be ornamental and undemanding. They owned a packaging business and David liked to say that the only thing they taught him was the importance of *wrapping things up nicely*. He left home at eighteen and got a job as a window dresser. He said for some years that he was going to be a theatre designer and then he got to the age where people stop talking about what they're going to become. This did not trouble him. He moved lightly through life, not expecting anchorage he'd never known.

One evening David's father mentioned Sandra.

Her parents were here for a drink last week. They said how nice it had been to see David in Berlin.

Berlin? Iris queried and then made herself say, Ah yes, Berlin.

She waited until they were in bed.

So when did you and Sandra go to Berlin?

She watched him scrambling to put an answer together.

We didn't go to Berlin.

Liar.

Not together. She needed some last-minute help. Surely you remember? It was work. Her parents were there to look after the boy. I went overnight or something. I was barely there, come to think of it. That big project. Surely you remember?

No, I don't remember. When was this?

89

Last year? The year before?

Which?

How should I know? It was one of the many tedious and badly paid little jobs I do that you show no interest in. You think I went there because I wanted to? For fun?

I think you went there to fuck Sandra.

You're mad.

Iris stopped listening. Her mind was scanning the last two years. She was in so much pain that she wanted to smash herself and so when David reached out and pulled her to him, she let him. More than that, she wanted him to.

We are bound together by dark patterns as well as light. We choose someone who makes us feel and so feeling arises and it can't all be good. David would turn her back on herself until she felt obliged to put her anger away. It was how he moved them past every crisis he provoked. But the pattern had worn itself out. Iris could not go through it again.

I want you to leave. You have to leave. Just leave.

Where am I supposed to go?

I don't know. Your sister's?

She had said this not knowing if she meant it. Such a pattern depends on those involved remaining within the bounds of their part. This makes the pattern particularly clear and so it becomes a way of steadying things that are not. It's familiar and predictable, and sometimes that's what is most required, however painful. But Iris had broken the pattern. Into what?

When they got home, David packed a bag and went to his sister's because that was where Iris told him to go. She assumed he'd be back in a week but when he returned it was to pack another bag. He considered the cramped house, his angry wife, his fractious daughters, the damp walls and warped doors, and left as soon as he could.

They settled into another pattern, with David spending two evenings a week at the house with Kate and Lou, which he presented as a favour to Iris. One weekend in three he took the girls to stay with his parents. Months passed and the relief he'd been feeling hardened into loneliness. He found he wasn't interested in sleeping with other women any more. He wanted Iris.

One day it seemed as if she wanted him too. She had to ask for his help because she had a migraine and could not so much as raise her head from the pillow. He'd come over and had a good day with the girls, bringing Iris exactly what she needed because he knew. He cleared up her vomit, put her in a bath, changed her nightclothes and sheets, and she did not feel ashamed because it was him. Then he lay down beside her and held her and she slept better than she had since he'd gone.

When she woke, she was still in his arms. He had been waiting to ask her something.

How long is this going to take?

What?

This punishment. I've done what you asked. Four months camping out at my sister's. I haven't lived with my children for four months. Isn't that enough?

It's not a question of—

I've been waiting, god knows why, for your permission to return and now—

But you haven't tried to restore anything. You haven't even wanted to talk.

About what? Sandra? Something that happened years ago?

But I only just found out about it. And it wasn't just Sandra, was it?

So what? You knew. We didn't talk about it but you knew.

In that moment she made herself look back on all she'd turned away from and there it was.

I'm not punishing you, she said.

What was the point in making me leave, then?

What you did was real. What it made me feel was real. What happens now has to be real.

She had not turned towards him but nor had she made any attempt to free herself. They continued to lie there, each waiting for the other to make something happen. Meanwhile another day began.

And then it was almost summer and Iris, who was so tired, was about to tell David to come back when she walked through a doorway beside a stranger and they turned towards each other and they said yes.

the interrupted city

Much of the city could be described as historical. There are buildings, monuments and other landmarks that have been here so long that no one questions their permanence. We make what use of them we can. We have repurposed our libraries, fire stations, churches, warehouses, butchers and pubs. We no longer require guildhalls, telephone boxes, docks or ballrooms and turn them into other things while still calling them what they were. We navigate the city by churches and fish markets just as we give emotions names that belong to a simpler time, if there ever was one.

There has been so little rain that autumn has begun already. The parks are yellow. Leaves start to collect in the streets. A desert wind brings a knife-edge of heat and fine red sand that's invisible in the air but coats every surface. People are burnt and thirsty and bored by the empty sky. They want the next thing to happen.

For weeks, Iris and Raif have been exchanging messages. He thanks her for showing him the cloud mirror and sends an article he's come across about another merman. He does not say that Helen has moved in. For Raif this is an aside. He only intends it to be a temporary solution. She's been living at the top of the house of friends who're getting divorced. And why not live together? As other men remark, women too, Helen is lovely.

When he hopes Iris is having a good summer, she mentions that she's never liked summer and that's it, they've interrupted themselves and enlarged their conversation. They settle into a rhythm of communicating every few days and the murmurs that underlie their correspondence – still about archives and accession numbers – start to be heard. *I want. I might. Will you. Could we. I can't stop thinking. I can't stop.*

The messages are a counterpoint to the disappointments of each day and the fears that are forming. *I want her to move out. I have to take him back.* They're afraid because something has been fixed. Iris cannot return to who she was before she met Raif and retreated from David. Raif cannot contemplate Helen without seeing Iris, however vaguely, behind her.

From up on the hill you can see that the city has no overall argument. It's not a series of avenues or a grid of blocks and so the best way to walk from one place to another is rarely obvious. Despite all the possibilities, most stick to a small number of paths which they follow with minor variations.

We follow paths we know too well to notice they are gone. Iris is walking over a bridge towards an office block she's known for thirty years and suddenly she isn't sure where it is. There are so many others now. And where did that gravel garden come from? Those trees? She takes her usual shortcut but meets a locked gate. She wonders if it has always been there, if she's imagined the shortcut and never noticed the gravel.

She's late and tries to make her way back to the bridge

but this place has never been a starting point. She doesn't know where to go. She gets out her phone and turns the map round and round. Where is she? A woman walks past and Iris almost asks her for help even though she can't believe she needs it. The woman was about to stop anyway because Iris looks so lost and, like anyone interrupted, so revealed.

the merman

In September, just as day and night are levelling, it rains for days. Across the land, towns are afloat and farms are at sea. The city was not designed for this recent weather of tempests and monsoons and so pipes erupt, roads are sheeted with water, gutters overflow. But most of the city's water remains hidden. It collects and moves slowly, if at all, along canals, sewers, and rivers that have sunk to gullies and then further into the earth. Yet it is water that opens up the city. When it rains, light spills.

Raif makes his way to the college pool, which is in the basement of a building that's to be sold the following year. The changing room is a clash of mildew and disinfectant. He touches as little as possible of the spongy matting and sticky wood, and climbs gingerly into the pool. It would surprise those who know him to see him in the water. He is sure, fast and strong, so absorbed and intent that other swimmers are forced to move round him. He swims length after length in an exalted state of pure momentum, which doesn't end when he gets out of the pool. He feels as if he's accelerating towards something he might describe as joy. Where this idea has come from, he will not yet admit. Outside it is still raining. He dresses without bothering to dry himself properly and cycles home in his shirt, taking his time and accepting every drop.

*

Iris stands by her open kitchen door, lights a cigarette and watches water splatter down the side of the house from a clump of matted green where some crack or block – she doesn't want to think about what exactly – has for a year or so caused this to happen. Brown suds are rising from the drain and when she opens the cupboard by the sink it releases a mouldy vapour. She looks up at the roof and down at the drain.

The museum is also prone to leaks and blockages. Water drips from light fittings and buckets are deployed. The work room in the stores, however, is temperature-controlled and windowless.

Iris enjoys the absence of time and weather, and the hours spent alone with a single object. Waiting for her in a plastic container in the laboratory sits the merman or *ningyo*. This one is somewhere between one and two hundred years old, and was obtained by a Dutch merchant at a fair in Japan. He has a fish's skin, bones and tail but dog's teeth, cat's claws and a face that is neither animal nor human. X-rays have given Iris some knowledge of his construction, confirming muddled layers of flesh and paper, and revealing the wire and nails that keep him in place.

There are *ningyo* who stand up and scream, and those, like this one, who crawl towards you on their bellies. His tail is negligible but he's hauling his heavily ribbed bulk forwards with powerful arms. His mouth is open wide and one taloned finger is raised but his intentions are unreadable. For all the detail of his teeth and claws, his eyes are a couple of empty whorls. The pale fur on his head, arms and back (fox or rabbit) gives him a senile or venerable air – not so much monkey as monkey god.

The merman has been in storage for twenty years and Iris has to recommend whether or not he can be put back on display. She's about to complete a conservation analysis and is worried about the varying requirements of skin, paper, metal, fur and bone. There are also dangers to be considered. If an object has elements of taxidermy then it may have been preserved with formaldehyde, or disinfected with arsenic or mercury when it arrived at the museum. The merman, intended to bring protection and luck, was probably poisonous. Iris does not find this ironic. It is a practical challenge.

His carton has been lined with chemically neutral packaging. Blocks of foam hold him in place and acid-free tissue has been used as extra protection and support. Though carefully contained, the merman has not been concealed. The wrapped object must remain visible so that the person unpacking it can see what they are about to touch.

The story was that if you ate the flesh of a *ningyo* you'd live forever but would eventually kill yourself out of boredom. Or that if you took a *ningyo* from the sea and held it captive, you'd be cursed. Or that there was a golden future ahead that would bring with it a deadly plague and only by possessing such a creature could you enjoy great prosperity while rendering yourself immune.

The merman is an example of what happens when different elements are forced together in an attempt to produce something magical. He belongs in the medical gallery alongside the surgical instruments, the dentist's chairs and the doctors' brass nameplates because he is a warning and the warning he gives is a kind of cure.

a crowded room

Helen is walking back into the party when she catches sight of Raif and his face lights up. She feels a pulse of delight just as she realises that it's not her he's looking at. She watches him walk towards the person who has thrown this switch: a small woman, not young, a solid presence in a plain white dress and flat shoes. While she looks un-remarkable, she draws the eye. She seems particularly clear and still.

The party, to launch a fellowship for which there is no sponsor as yet, is in a large plain room in one of the central colleges. It's full of people who know each other and who've come straight from work. Helen is feeling out of place in her salmon-pink velvet dress, her stilettos and bouncy blow-dried hair. She has just spent a long time in the Ladies, studying herself under feeble light. The only other women who have dressed up as much as she are younger. They've been brought along by men who have no conception of this as a date and who are locked into conversation with each other. These women stand along-side Helen at the mirror and take their time adding to their already overdone faces.

Helen is tall and tapering and widely admired but now she rounds her shoulders and watches Raif. He and the woman don't kiss hello, the woman doesn't even smile, but Raif is grinning and standing up taller. He says something in the woman's ear and she laughs and puts a hand on his arm as she introduces him to her group.

This is a chance meeting in a room in which both Iris and Raif belong. They're on common ground and so feel a little released. Raif can walk towards Iris without hesitation and she can claim him. In the conversation that follows, they give the impression of knowing each other well. She recalls how he almost dropped the cloud mirror out of a window. He counters that he caught her as she fell down the station steps. They don't look at each other but stand side by side, similar in their posture, Helen notes, as if announcing that they are of a kind.

Such attractions are being played out elsewhere in the room and on the whole they mean nothing. A man is talking to one woman while his body twists towards another. A student has placed herself in her tutor's eyeline, unaware that she keeps patting her hair and licking her lips as she pretends to listen to her date. A man has placed his hand on his boyfriend's shoulder as if stopping him tipping into the arms of the person they've just met.

These are signals rather than messages. Helen knows this. She's read about it and discussed it with friends, and she can tell that the man and woman she's standing beside are surely having an affair. Why else are they being so attentive to each other's partners, smiling to the extent of baring their teeth? She knows what it is to catch the blast of someone's attention or to feel a taut line to them wherever they are in a room.

Even though she realises that it's not a good idea, Helen

walks over to Raif. He takes a long moment to acknowl-edge her and when he does, he introduces her by both name and surname, like a colleague, so that a woman – not the one in the white dress – says that Raif has been com-plaining about departmental politics and are they as awful as he says?

I don't know. I'm not. I'm—

She wants to say *Raif's girlfriend* (or partner?) and he might say *We moved in together last week*, and there would be a round of warm congratulations. But the woman who addressed her isn't interested. She was just being polite and the conversation has rolled on. Raif is at his best. Iris says little but seems at ease. She doesn't look at Helen, who is willing her to do so. Close up, Helen realises that Iris is possibly older than Raif and that she is a force. Her plain dress, her hair, are background.

Someone taps Iris on the shoulder so that she turns out of the group and – hand on his arm again – takes Raif with her into a new tight knot. Those remaining consider Helen. One says firmly how lovely it was to meet her as they fade away. Iris introduces Raif to the director of her museum, who says hello and moves on.

During the brief time in which Raif and Iris are alone, they hand each other a key. He begins.

You alright?

Just about. You?

Neither is suffering. This is how they tell each other that there's a quieter connection to be made.

Oh, I'm fine, he says. But it's so crowded—

Yes, she says. It is.

Raif wants to intensify whatever this is, to have something to hold onto and carry home.

Are we talking about life or this room?

Or life as a room?

She means to deflect him but he likes this idea and pursues it.

So if your life were a room, what would it—

Walls, she interrupts him. It would be four walls – no windows or doors – gradually closing in.

They are looking so directly at each other that neither is aware of it.

What about you? she asks. What's the first thing I'd see in your so-called room?

My broken heart.

Iris is so surprised and so moved that she's unable to respond before the tall woman in the pink dress reinserts herself. She looks as if she has something urgent to say so Iris smiles and waits.

I'd like another glass of wine, Helen says specifically to Raif.

He doesn't look at her as he replies.

Then get one.

Helen takes a step back. Raif picks up his earlier conversation with Iris.

So the model is on display at the moment?

Yes. I believe it's the largest Auzoux made in the Normandy factory.

I've seen some of the moulds in Cambridge. The starfish, the fern, the May beetle . . .

Helen is still there, trying to find a way in.

Model of what?

A horse, Iris explains.

You mean like a toy?

No, an anatomical model.

Didn't they teach anatomy through dissection?

Yes, but—

Another person taps Iris on the shoulder, she greets them, and when she turns back Raif and Helen have gone.

On her way home Iris concludes that Helen is a colleague who has a crush on Raif. He was being polite but was clearly thrown by her persistence. Iris is pleased with her own gracious behaviour in letting her twice join their conversation.

Helen is driving them home.

So did you enjoy that? Raif asks, leaning back and shutting his eyes.

Yes. Although I didn't really know who anyone was and so it was all a bit—

I did warn you.

But you could have—

You should take the next left. There are roadworks along here.

She knows there's nothing to be gained by saying anything. This is something else she's read about and discussed. She knows how he will react and that she will still say it.

When I came over. I mean when you were talking to that woman. The one in the white dress. The thing is, I could see why they all thought I was your colleague. You introduced me as if you barely knew me. I mean I felt like a stranger who'd just walked up and stood beside you.

Perhaps it's not such a good idea for you to come to my work events. Not if you don't enjoy them.

But I would enjoy myself if you'd just—

Just what?

You seemed uncomfortable.

I thought you said that you were the one who felt uncomfortable.

I know. I did. But I was because you were.

I was or I seemed?

Helen has been redirected from a large room to a small one where they will pick over words – something he is good at. She makes herself stop talking.

The traffic has come to a halt. It's after rush hour and before pub closing on a weekday, yet these last two miles will take as long as the rest of the journey. The lights turn green but no one moves. Helen watches three girls sitting on a bench reading and writing messages on their phones. She can't tell if they're best friends or total strangers. Beside them a man is turning small circles, one hand reaching towards passers-by. Is he asking for money or that they keep him from falling? He doesn't bother the girls, who sit there in a force field of youth.

Raif knows that he's hurt Helen but not how. He reaches for her hand and she pulls away. The gesture was too deliberate. What does she want? For him to take her hand without planning to first. How can he achieve this?

He'd taken her to the party hoping that if he presented them as a couple to the world, he'd be able to convince himself. He stood there, trying to be the man who arrived with Helen and failing. Then he'd seen Iris and switched himself on, walked over and made a small claim, which she reciprocated.

something is pressing

From three brief meetings Iris has built an idea of Raif that she considers complete, and the sharp tone in which he spoke to Helen at that party has no place in it. She pushes the memory away but it will float back. Meanwhile he stands in her mind, isolated and simplified. He is something in outline, what exactly she can't say.

One evening she and Max take beer up onto the roof of the stores. Iris hasn't mentioned David for several weeks and Max is curious. Iris evidently wants to talk about something and it seems not to be David.

I went to that party, she begins. It turned out to be quite interesting.

You met someone.

Not really.

What's his name?

Why is that the first thing people ask? About dogs and babies and other people. It doesn't tell you anything.

Of course it does.

Iris wants Raif in the air but not fixed there. She won't say his name. She brought up the party so that she could see what it was like to mention him and now that she has, there's no need to say any more. Only something is pressing.

There was someone with him, or who knew him.

A partner?

No. I don't know. At least, he didn't seem pleased. The way he spoke to her—

What did he say?

She said she wanted a drink. Like it was an announcement and he was supposed to do something about it.

His date, at least. How did he respond?

He didn't, really.

But you just said something about how he spoke to her.

Did I?

Iris has arrived at the detail that keeps placing itself in front of everything else.

I think he's a bit awkward.

Rude?

He was nervous and – I don't know – logical.

Like you, you mean.

He was like that when he came to the museum.

When was that?

Didn't I say?

No, you didn't.

The point is it was ages ago and we barely met but we met again. And before that, actually.

I see.

Iris and Max have had many conversations along these lines. Iris offers evidence of something that she doesn't, in the end, want to acknowledge. Her friend is quick to formulate and Iris just as quick to deflect. It's as if she's being given pieces of a puzzle that she lays out face down. Max offers another part of the puzzle.

How's David?

David? He's alright. I think.

Still at his sister's?

I suppose so. Yes.

But how is he really?

Alright. As far as I know.

It's a terrible disease.

It's more of a diagnosis.

But he had those episodes.

That's what I mean. Most of the time he's fine.

It is Iris who brings the conversation back to Raif and she's annoyed with herself for doing so. Described out loud, what she thought of as an enlivening tension sounds so girlish.

I do wonder, she says, what he meant.

Max is still worrying about David.

Who? Oh. Meant by what?

By giving me his card and getting in touch and sending me all these messages.

You write back?

I do. It's a good conversation.

How often?

I don't know. Quite often. Most days.

Most days?

Iris looks worried.

Is there something wrong with that?

This is a real question. She likes to do things properly but is often unsure what this might mean.

Nothing's wrong with it as it is, says Max. It's just a conversation. Only where's it leading?

Does it have to lead anywhere?

Do you want it to?

Iris doesn't reply. Max tries again.

What did you feel when you first saw him?

I recognised him.

He reminded you of someone?

I don't think so.

So what did you recognise?

I don't know.

It'll be something basic. The way he raised his hand or turned his head. It'll have reminded you of something. Come on, think about it.

I'm not going to think about it.

But Iris is thinking about it all the time.

Iris and Max are drinking on the roof because it's one of David's evenings with the girls. He orders pizza and they watch an episode of a show he thinks they like. No one enjoys it but that's not the point. Sitting there together puts them back into a familiar arrangement. Then the girls go to bed and he sits on without them.

David's life is one of empty shapes. He's a father, a husband, a designer and a patient but none of these in any substantial way. He despises himself for chasing sex, not making money, failing his wife, upsetting his children and being ill, and for not knowing how to solve any of it. There are things he wants to say to Iris but he's so tired.

Up in the attic Lou is awake but she lies there quietly so as not to disturb her sister. She's thinking. Things she has long felt are coming into view now that she has the words for them.

Children's emotions circulate like breath or blood. They cannot be grasped or suppressed because they have not been named. When children are too young to use the words, their parents describe their feelings for them. Now Lou has the words and her feelings are gathering. She needs to say something.

how a heart is broken

Raif was fourteen when his father was killed. The collision happened at night in heavy rain at a dangerous junction on the edge of town. A young mother in the other car died too and while the investigation cleared Raif's father of all blame, many in the town turned away from the family from then on.

His two uncles flew in and his mother, Bridget, asked if Raif wanted to go with them to see his father's body. She looked worried but she was nodding and so he nodded too. When he came home she thanked him for going.

I'm sure it was hard but it will help you in the long run. To process it all. And your uncles will tell the family. It'll mean a lot to the family.

This was what she said when coaxing him into writing thank-you letters and birthday cards. Now she was coaxing him into being proud of having gone with his uncles to that appalling nothing-coloured room where his father lay with a sheet tucked so high and tight across his chest that for a moment Raif had thought that all that was left of him was a head on a pillow. They were there for an hour and he tried to weep and pray like his uncles, when they did.

At school, boys passed him carefully while girls showed a new interest. The word they used when approaching him was *tragic. Really tragic.* Then everyone forgot about what had happened until one day the queen of the girls said something about having never seen a dead body.

I have, said Raif.

You have what?

Seen a dead body.

What was it like? asked a boy who was the only one not to recall at that moment that Raif's father had died two weeks earlier.

Not like anything, really.

The group waited.

Did you see him? Your dad? After?

The queen of the girls put her hand on his arm as she said this, causing such an eruption of desire that when he spoke it sounded as if he were finding the words too painful to utter.

My uncles flew thousands of miles to pray over the body. They wore black. It is our custom.

If his father had heard him speak like that he would have laughed.

When Raif told people that his father had been an architect, they assumed he'd grown up in a house of glass. The few friends he'd taken home were surprised by the bungalow which, although quite large and white and modern in its way, lacked character. When he brought Liis down for the first time, she'd shown no interest in the house or his childhood room or the photo albums. Bridget told the family stories. Liis went early to bed.

Do you think she's bored? he asked his mother.

For Bridget, as for Raif, everything about Liis was explained by her father's defection.

I should think she's in shock.

Raif envisaged the moment of the decision to stay in New York and Liis, so young, the stakes so high, frozen inside it. He didn't tell his mother that he was no longer sure that the moment belonged to her.

Liis was not supposed to die. They'd only just started on the discussion of treatment options but it was as if she made a private decision to accelerate her illness. There was a horrible smoothness to the way things progressed. The scope of her days diminished neatly until she lay in a state not unlike sleep. Her hospice room had a glass screen behind which was a bed for Raif. The glass was intended to encourage him to rest without fearing that he had lost sight of her. Such an arrangement felt quite familiar. He found it easy to relax.

Afterwards, he went to talk to a therapist.

Your father didn't want you to learn Arabic?

He didn't speak Arabic. That was his father. His mother spoke Japanese. I don't. We spoke a bit of French. I learnt it anyway at school.

Tell me about school.

I wasn't popular.

Because you were foreign?

What? No. Because I didn't know how to . . .

How to fit in?

How to be.

Were there incidents?

No. Yes. None that made any particular impact.

What are you feeling?

I'm in pain, I think.

You think?

That is, I don't feel a lot.

It was as much as he knew.

It took him days to make himself contact Liis's family. The number was right there in her book, listed under her surname – Must. *Least Most*, he liked to call her, pleased with the paradoxical qualities of this although she was the kind of person no one teased or conferred with a nickname. Unlike the girls he'd grown up with, she was never silly and never sweet.

The woman who answered the phone said that she was Liis's sister. (A sister?) She asked for no more information than Raif offered.

I'm sorry, he said. I'm very sorry. But it was alright. She didn't suffer. I know it's a cliché but she just fell asleep and didn't wake up.

A cliché?

I meant that it was what we all hope for. The best we can hope for. She just let go.

OK.

I know she spoke to your mother only last week.

My mother.

I think so, yes.

Thank you for calling.

Is there somewhere she'd like to be? Her ashes. A place, I mean. Somewhere she liked to be.

There's no need.

Please. I have to.

As you wish.

Ashamed not to know the sister's name, he did not ask. He was back on the ice, reluctant to take a step towards his dead wife's story for fear of what it might reveal.

I'm not, I don't feel

The gradual development of their relationship has led Raif to think that Helen moving in would be another gentle adjustment. But as he enters the flat each evening, a weight slides into place. Helen notices.

Has something happened?

I'm not, I don't feel—

He's coming home not to Helen but to Liis, someone he felt unauthorised to touch, who served food he couldn't taste. Her silence, even more than her illness, was what weighed on him. Liis has been dead for two years and here is someone new offering him all the things he craved from her but here, too, is the weight.

He thinks he loved Liis in spite of her remoteness. In ten years' time he'll be walking down the street when he'll be struck by the realisation that it was in fact why. By then he'll understand what he is drawn to – a withholding that balances something similar in himself – but he doesn't know this yet. He comes home to Helen, bumps into furniture, gets headaches and turns away.

He is frightened too, although this is another thing he doesn't feel. He'll find out, surely, that Helen is no more real than Liis. She'll discard veil after veil until she disappears. Perhaps women are no more than a series of veils?

*

Helen wants to mark the anniversary of meeting Raif but she's not sure what really counts. So she waits and when it's a year to the day she first stayed the night, she sees the bottle of champagne in the fridge and realises that he has remembered. So she places a CD of her favourite songs on his pillow and says that she will make them a special meal.

She's lit the candles and Raif has just taken his place at the table when the doorbell rings. Emily, Ashley and Jessica bustle in, talking all at once about the day they've had shopping and how they just need to leave their bags and get changed and then they'll be off, no bother at all. Ashley is first into the kitchen where Helen, wearing a smart new apron, is holding a spoon in one hand and a saucepan in the other.

It's her! A domestic goddess as well as a nympho scientist, says Jessica.

We chose well.

Helen isn't sure which of them says it, perhaps all three. *We chose well.*

Emily goes to the fridge and pulls out the bottle of wine that Helen has been chilling. Jessica is getting three more glasses from a cupboard. Ashley looks around.

I think we're interrupting something.

You are, says Helen.

She doesn't mean to sound rude but, damn it, they are.

Raif does not react. He introduces his cousins and explains that he took them to her play. Helen is delighted and waits for them to say something about the performance, only they don't. They talk to Raif. It's as if Helen's not there; the candles, the curry, the flowers not there. She has the same sensation she had at the party when Raif was talking to Iris: that she's been left outside a circle and that he hasn't noticed or doesn't care. This time she will step in and stay in. She thinks of something to say.

I'm going away tomorrow.

I'm going to an all-day meeting about the new maths curriculum, says Jessica.

And I'm going to the dentist, says Emily.

Poor you, says Raif.

It's really quite an interesting job, says Helen. You see, I'm going to be—

Emily interrupts her.

Raif, do you eat curry these days? Because there was that time on holiday—

That's right! You lay on the bathroom floor all night.

It's a training course for magistrates, Helen persists. I'm going to role-play people in court.

We should be getting ready, says Ashley, standing up.

Some days I'll play a barrister, says Helen, others a defendant.

Ashley, who hasn't said that she's a police officer, laughs.

Is there a way to play a defendant, then? Were you taught that at drama school? How to play guilty, how to play innocent?

Of course not. Not in a general way. I'm given character outlines, the context.

Jessica, the mathematician, joins in.

Talking of defendants, someone's invented a new algorithm for detecting serial killers.

What exactly is an algorithm? asks Helen.

This time they all laugh. Helen's not stupid. She knows roughly what the word refers to. She's just trying to show an interest.

Clearly I'm only smart enough to chop lemongrass, she says.

The triplets do not modify themselves easily. They have refused to notice how they're making Helen feel but now that she has been curt with them, they're alert. They look at her and at each other and then stand up.

Stay for another drink, Raif says to them. Please.

It's challenging work, says Helen as if she's just remembered something.

Chopping lemongrass? one of them says.

All three give the same ugly snort of laughter but Helen pushes on.

You have to memorise enough facts about each case to be able to improvise.

I've chipped my nail polish, says Jessica.

I'll be away for a month, says Helen as they top up their glasses, finishing the bottle.

Maths and manicures – what a life! says Raif.

Still he has not looked at Helen.

The triplets head off again to the bedroom – or is it the bathroom? They seem to be everywhere at once. Helen contemplates the curry and waits. Raif sits back and opens the newspaper.

Something smells good.

I am not your wife, thinks Helen. *I am not a woman who spends all afternoon chopping lemongrass to make you happy. This is a special occasion. It is* my *occasion.*

Dinner can wait till we've got the place to ourselves again, she says. They're just dropping some stuff off, aren't they?

They'll stay for a drink.

They've just had one.

Raif hasn't heard sharpness from Helen before. Now he looks up.

I hardly ever see them and they're almost the only family I have. They're the reason you and I met. It was their idea, you see. We should thank them.

Someone is playing music and someone else is speaking loudly into their phone. It's as if there are thirty of them, thinks Helen, not three. Half an hour later they reappear.

That smells delicious, they say without enthusiasm.

Would you like some? Raif says. I'm sure it will stretch.

It won't, says Helen. Sorry. If I'd known you were coming then of course—

Raif looks upset.

At least let's have another drink.

He goes to the fridge.

We have champagne! Let's celebrate.

Celebrate what?

Helen waits for Raif to say *It's a year since Helen and I met* but he doesn't.

I know, he says, let's drink to . . . to . . . Thursdays.

The triplets dance round the kitchen swigging champagne and toasting Thursdays until Helen says that it's a Tuesday.

That's the point! Raif shouts in a new silly voice.

Ashley puts her glass down.

No offence but this champagne tastes like shit. To be honest.

Don't be so rude! shout Emily and Jessica together.

I don't mind, shrugs Raif. It's just something I won in a charity raffle at work. I've been wondering who to palm it off on.

Helen takes off her apron.

I've got a headache, she says, so I think I'll just go and lie down. It was nice to . . .

They seem not to notice her leaving the room.

The walls of the flat are thin and as she lies there she can hear the triplets quizzing Raif.

Does she live here?

No, she's just between places.

That's what they all say.

Raif makes some sort of noise in response.

Eventually they leave. Raif helps himself to the curry and takes a long time coming to bed. He can see that the triplets have reservations about Helen. Is it too soon? How long will she stay? The weight slides into place.

Later they're woken by the triplets coming back for their bags and figuring out that they won't make the last train home. They sleep, with practised ease, in a row on the sofa bed which, when open, fills most of the room.

a blade

The lancet is the tool with which we prise ourselves apart. It's a way of doing what the eye would like to: piercing surfaces and isolating detail so as to hold it up to the light. We do this even to the eye itself.

First we used our teeth and nails, and then sharpened reeds, bamboo and thorns. We adapted mussel shells and shark's teeth. We carved blades from flint, obsidian and jade, and forged them from iron and steel following the lines of hunting knives, chisels and swords.

More recently, operations were confident and majestic. Those born in the mid-twentieth century bear scars that sweep across the belly, back and chest. Now much is done through keyhole surgery, and using light and sound rather than blades. *Today, as minimally invasive techniques, endoscopes, laser and ultrasound sources evolve, many hallowed incisions of surgical access diminish in length or disappear entirely* ... We have lost our scars and so forget that the body has been disturbed and that while a problem may have been solved, the solution will leave its trace.

our best selves

Iris understands her connection with Raif. It has reminded her of a certain capacity in herself but she knows that this has nothing to do with who he really is – or she – and that it will pass. The oppressive summer made everything seem overheated. She was gripped by their whispering messages but all that has subsided now.

The yes, the waking, the following, meeting and whispering do not necessarily lead anywhere. Sometimes all that's needed from an encounter with a stranger is a reminder of your best self. If they see only what shines, you remember that there is a perfect version. They expect the best of you and so this is what you offer and you thank them for it. You might even fall in love.

Lou has turned twelve and David takes the girls to the cinema with four friends while Iris prepares a birthday tea. How to fit all those girls round the table? And David. That makes eight and there are only four chairs. She and David can stand. The girls will like that, the grown-ups not joining in, but there are still six of them. Iris steps out into her dingy garden and brings in the chairs, which are rickety and crusted with lichen.

The front door opens and the girls clatter in. The four friends hover, nibbling their fingernails and twiddling their hair. They're wearing nail polish and lots of necklaces and the same skinny jeans, T-shirt and trainers as Lou and Kate.

Iris looks again at the table and sees that she's made a birthday tea for eight-year-olds and not what these self-conscious and wary creatures might expect. She's baked and iced the animal biscuits she always makes. There are mini-pizzas, chocolate buttons, strawberries, celery and carrot and dips, and a large bowl of crisps. There are also three kinds of ice cream in the freezer, and she was up half the night making a cake covered in butter-flies because six months ago Kate and Lou had a craze on butterfly hairclips. Now they both wear their hair scraped into a knot like their friends.

Iris points at the garden chairs.

Kate, Lou, I've put you there and there.

A look passes between them – the garden chairs? – but they sit down. The guests hover, waiting for Iris to tell them where to sit too but at that moment her phone buzzes in her pocket. (When did she start carrying it around?)

Sit down, everyone, help yourselves.

She strides out of the room. David, Kate and Lou are used to Iris not explaining herself. She is often curt and they know she doesn't mean to be rude but the guests are wondering what's wrong. When she comes back they're still waiting to start. A year ago no one would have waited. They'd have been helping themselves to the chocolate buttons and biscuits, and heaping crisps onto their plates.

I told you to start.

She means it as an apology for keeping them waiting but

it sounds like an order. Kate passes round the carrots and Lou the dip. Each child takes a small amount.

Iris is smiling to an unusual degree.

Were you looking at something funny? asks Kate. On your phone? Was it funny?

Lou fixes her sister with a look and a quick shake of the head. She knows not to ask this kind of question but she doesn't yet understand why. Her shifting self has acquired a new sense of atmosphere. She detects tides and currents, electricity and clouds, and sees that her mother and father ignore them and so she is trying to do the same.

It was obviously important, David says tightly, or Mum wouldn't have left the table.

For fuck's sake, David.

Iris says this quite ordinarily and it's another thing her family are used to. The other girls are impressed but Kate and Lou move quickly to divert an argument. They are practised at this.

What was it, Mum?

Was it funny, Mum?

It was a merman.

A mermaid?

She said a mer*man*, corrects the smallest visitor.

Is it real? asks the tallest.

Iris is careful not to smile.

If you mean real in the way mermaids are real, then yes.

Can we see it? the tallest girl asks. The funny picture?

Iris clicks on the attachment Raif has sent her. It is not of the merman in her museum but another, which he has been writing about. The girls pass it round in silence. It's neither scary nor comical enough for them to know how to respond. David passes the phone without looking.

Is this what you do? asks the littlest guest. Do you look after a merman?

This is a question Kate and Lou would never ask. They take for granted that their mother works in a museum and that she is a conservator. They know that this means mending things. They've visited the museum plenty of times and have seen all there is to see but now their friend is interested.

Can we see the merman, Mum? asks Kate.

This one's not at my museum but we do have one.

But can we see it?

Of course. Only I'm working on it at the moment so it's not on public display.

But we're not public so can we see it?

Iris is pleased by their interest but confused by the fact that it has been prompted by a message from Raif.

No one can see it while I'm working on it. Not even you.

There had been a bubble of excitement, of the girls having something to offer their friends, and she has ruined it.

But of course, as soon as it's ready, you'll be the very first.

It's not really real, though, is it? says Lou in punishment.

No, it's not. It's more real than real in that we need to . . . we all need . . .

They wait for her to say more.

It's a metaphor, isn't it? says the littlest guest so quietly that she appears to be talking to herself.

Exactly, Iris says. A metaphor of how we're made. And our fears.

Mum, you're being weird, says Lou.

So weird that I made you a cake. It's the usual botch, of course, but at least I made it.

She produces the butterfly cake. Kate and Lou maintain a rigidly neutral expression until the littlest guest, the one they most want to be their friend, claps her hands and exclaims *Butterflies!* They all clap while David takes the cake and carries it to the table and Lou stands to blow out her twelve candles. Iris reaches for her phone to take a picture – a precious picture of her girl on her birthday – and what is she thinking about? Whether or not Raif noticed the girls' photo on her phone when he picked it up for her at the station. If he assumed that she's married. (She is.)

When the girls go off to watch another film, David helps clear the table. No one has eaten more than a couple of mouthfuls of cake. Iris is not a cook and while she has modelled some beautiful butterflies, the cake itself is greasy and dry. David stacks the plates too carelessly and drops them, smashing three. Iris gives a small sigh, a habit that has enraged David for years.

I'm sorry, alright? I'm sorry my coordination is fucked and my nerves are fucked. My brain is full of holes, remember?

With that the frail triumph of the birthday tea collapses. Iris wants to go and sit with her daughters but they no longer require her. She's about to open the back door and have a cigarette when the doorbell rings.

That'll be Martin, she says to David. He's dropping them all off. Could you answer?

Me? I'm just a guest.

I can't—

What? Say hello to Martin?

David goes to the door to see the visitors out. When he comes back Iris manages to thank him, refusing to notice that this is agony for him, this coming home and having to leave again. Most of the time David feels turned inside out by the pain. Sitting with his daughters he is put right and now he's about to be turned inside out again.

He thinks Iris is cold and somewhere in herself she agrees with him. She feels no pity, only irritation and a deep animal contempt for his weakness. She keeps herself busy till he leaves and then sits on the back doorstep smoking and contemplating her stalled attempts at a garden. The erupted paving slabs are puddled with moss and the narrow strip where she lifted them to create a flowerbed is full of mildewed weeds and cat shit. She keeps meaning to put the slabs back.

Now and then she looks at the image of the merman Raif sent and eventually she sends a reply.

Is he a warning or a cry for help?

It takes some time for Raif, working his way through student essays while Helen mends a light socket, to grasp what she's referring to. It's as if he doesn't know he sent her the merman or has somehow forgotten.

Martin is the father of the tallest girl. Some years ago he invited David to a Sunday-morning football game on the common and they became friends too. The two families spent time together but there was always a certain unease.

Have you got a problem with Martin? David asked Iris.

We don't have much to say.

She wasn't interested in who Martin was. She found him dull while he found her frightening. The reason they were reserved in each other's company was because they had a sexual similarity which both recognised. It was dangerous.

One night they met at a friend's birthday drinks. Iris was alone because Kate and Lou had chickenpox and David stayed to look after them. Martin's wife was just home from hospital with their third child. Iris felt a migraine starting, as it always did with a pain behind her left eye, but she was desperate to get out of the house.

I'm cooking for us, David announced as she left. So be back by eight thirty.

She hadn't said she would.

Martin was the first person she spoke to. Nothing interesting was said but they enjoyed each other. At half past eight, Iris said she should be going and Martin offered her a lift. When they got outside, his car wouldn't start.

Shall we call a cab? she asked.

He looked down the street as if towards his wife, his children, the new baby and all they required of him, before telling Iris that he'd call a cab for her but he should stay and get someone to jump-start the car. Iris, also looking down the street, insisted on staying too. When they finally set off, Iris remembered something.

Will we go past a late-night chemist? I meant to pick up some migraine pills on the way here.

You need them tonight?

I think I might.

Well, I need to run the car for a good while anyway so let's go and find some.

It was as if they'd been handed the script for a spontaneous act. Martin could think of nothing more exciting than driving round the city with Iris. He knew he understood her better than her husband did. David called her Iris of the Many Walls. Martin saw no walls.

They were giggly and animated and so unlike the careful selves who met on doorsteps and over Sunday lunches, when they made sure they didn't so much as brush against one another in passing. Now, arriving at a chemist an hour's drive from home, they held hands as they rushed in. David wouldn't have recognised this boisterous, leaping version of Iris. He'd never met her.

By the time Martin pulled up outside her house, it was almost midnight. They hadn't really tried to find the way back and travelled miles across the city in the wrong direction, finding themselves on the overpass and seeing every exit just a little too late. Even now Iris didn't hurry to get out of the car. They talked a little more and she kissed him on the cheek, leaning against him for a moment. As she approached the house, pain started to cage her head and she welcomed it.

Three streets away Martin stepped into his dark home, relieved that his wife was sleeping. In the morning he would be his amiable, detached self – the man out of armour everyone took him for. The next Sunday, on the common, he came over to David to apologise. He'd felt bad that Iris stayed while he got the car started and so it seemed only fair to help her find those pills. He'd had no idea it would turn into such a quest. He presumed David had heard the whole story but Iris had said nothing. Martin told it anxiously, in too much detail. David listened, all the while envisaging Martin and Iris having sex in the car in some side street. He made a point of being as friendly as ever to Martin while ensuring that he and Iris were not left alone again.

Lou was pleased with her party and relieved that her parents had behaved well. She'd decided not to complain about having to let Kate join in. The other girls had said her sister was very grown-up for her age. But she, Lou, was the one whose body and mind had started to unanchor. Some days she woke up feeling as if she were underwater. Other days she was a genius superhero. All this internal activity thrilled and drained her. She wanted to worry about her parents but she didn't have the energy. She watched them perform being her parents for her friends and wondered when she would learn to do likewise – to be able to be her best self whenever necessary and to know when not to speak or think or look.

It was one of those evenings when Iris forgot to come up and say goodnight. Being in the attic meant that the girls could anyway stay up as late as they chose, providing they were quiet. They often communicated through gestures. Not speaking was becoming a way of giving each other a bit of space. Lou watched as Kate put something in the cupboard by her bed. When the door was shut again, she went and sat down beside her and raised her hands in a questioning shrug. Kate turned the matter over and then unlocked the cupboard. For years it had been a motley sort of doll's house but now it had been cleared. There was a single item on the top shelf. Their father had left the cable for his phone charger at the house that afternoon and here it was, carefully coiled. Lou took her time in contemplating this. Then she went to her desk and wrote something on a scrap of paper and handed it to Kate, who placed it precisely beside the cable. It was a date and a number.

They both woke early and this was when they talked.

I don't think David should be drinking, said Lou.

Or Iris.

But she hasn't got a diagnosis.

Lou, what if she has but she doesn't know or she's just not telling us?

Lou deflects this anxiety by moving the conversation on. It's something else she knows she has to learn how to do.

She thinks we want David to move back in.

For a long moment neither speaks.

Do you actually? says Kate in the end.

Only now does Lou realise what she feels.

I dunno.

But he's not well so we have to say yes. We're family.

But is he actually?

What? Not well or family?

the sting

In their last year of living together, David insisted on taking Iris out once a month or so to a bad local restaurant. He said it was proof of his desire to make things work. Iris came to dread it. He would sit opposite her, wary and monosyllabic, as if she were about to hand over the results of a test. One night they were sitting in the restaurant's garden. The tables had been pushed too closely together and she became aware that the people on either side were fascinated by her and David's silence. She saw them glancing over and started to talk warmly to David, wanting to prove them wrong, but he looked back at her as if he too were a stranger. He had a gift for exempting himself.

Iris screamed. There'd been something on her arm and she'd tried to brush it off. It was a bee and it stung her, which hurt but not so much that she should have cried out as she did. The man on her right turned to her immediately, took some ice from their jug of water, wrapped it in a napkin and gave it to her to press against the sting. Her arm was swelling badly. Someone produced an antihistamine.

It was only a bee sting but everyone in that garden was upset by it.

You poor thing, they said. Does it hurt? Are you alright?

Iris said that she was fine, it was nothing. David sipped his wine and watched.

When they got home he came into the bathroom where she was putting cream on her arm.

Did you have to involve the entire restaurant? Those poor people were trying to have a quiet night out and you staged such a drama that they felt obliged to rescue you. It was a sting. It didn't even hurt all that much, did it. I've never felt so embarrassed.

It doesn't matter, she said. We won't be going there again.

The man on Iris's right had been very attentive but she knew that she was getting the best of him. We start with our best selves. Had the woman he was with been stung like that, David would have leapt about finding ice and she would have been like Iris – smiling and grateful and dismissive of her pain.

They would linger, best self to best self, as if polishing the moment so as to have something shiny to take home: a shield to raise against the dull person you live with, to dazzle them with what you are capable of, to warn them.

an anatomical model of a horse

Here is a body that can be taken apart and put back together without evident damage. So not exactly lifelike. It has no surface and so there is nothing to pierce in order to reach its inner workings but the glossy raw red of its muscles repels even now. Who would want to touch a creature with no skin? We do our best to retain our surfaces.

Visitors to the museum take for granted that the horse is still intact after a hundred and fifty years. At the time it was made, anatomy lessons depended on corpses, which quickly decayed, or wax models, which were easily damaged. The horse is made out of paper, glue, cork and clay. Each part was mass-produced in a lead mould by the leading manufacturer of anatomical and botanical models in France at that time: Louis Thomas Jérôme Auzoux. He demonstrated his models at the Great Exhibition of 1851, eleven years before Goddard arrived with his cloud mirror.

Auzoux was living in the last years of the great age of horses. He made this model look as real as he could but scale was a practical matter. His horse is only half-life-size, waist-high to most visitors. They had, without knowing it, envisaged the horses they knew: in fields, on plinths, among the pages of storybooks – either majestic or in miniature and always elegant, unlike this thing whose size brought to mind a large sheep or dog.

Auzoux's horse is a subject for investigation whose parts are already labelled. It remains clear. It is not the horse we know. It is not the real thing.

an understanding of its parts

Iris was preparing to give a talk on the horse as part of the museum's autumn lunchtime series. This may have been why she'd mentioned it to Raif. She sent him the flyer and he replied that he looked forward to it.

She enters the museum's modest lecture theatre and finds herself with an audience of ten. There are three women in their sixties or seventies, four postgraduate students, someone from the museum's education department, and a tall woman with heavy glasses and heavy hair. Iris cannot make her out but beside her is Raif. There are empty seats to either side of them which means they've chosen to sit together which means he brought her with him and what does that mean?

Iris has thirty-six images, mostly pertaining to the model's construction. She has analysed the clay that Auzoux added to the papier-mâché to make it more durable as well as the stability of the egg tempera used to pick out muscle tissue and arteries. She has researched fully the technical and commercial reasons for building the model at half-life-size.

She planned to extemporise from notes, to keep it light and sparkling, but she's thrown by Raif's presence and affronted by the woman in glasses. So she reads the points she's prepared and fails in each case to think of something further to say. She is finished in twenty minutes, having repeated one point twice because the woman took off her glasses and shook out her hair.

Raif's face is fixed in the smallest possible smile, which Iris thinks at first is friendly then amused then pitying. The woman's holding her phone and seems to be recording the talk, which makes Iris stumble all the more. How lazy and rude, she thinks, while noticing that Raif isn't bothering to take notes either. Finally Iris asks if there are any questions. Four hands are raised, including the woman's.

Iris smiles at someone else, who introduces herself as a professor of veterinary science.

I myself found anatomical models useful, of course, and one can admire the specificity of Auzoux's beast. But as an instrument of learning, is it not a blizzard of detail?

The woman with the glasses is nodding. Raif gives no indication of his view.

Before Iris can decide what to say, and she's determined on an impressive response, someone answers the question for her.

But didn't Auzoux's labelling make it possible for the student to learn at their own pace? He numbered each part so that the student was guided by the order in which the animal should be dissected.

The woman with the glasses speaks next. She has a charming elusive accent, so everyone is listening, but her gaze wanders. She seems to be speaking to the air.

You take something apart and put it together over and over, learning the names for each component and how they fit. You accrue detail rather than attempt to absorb it all at once.

There are noises of approval but the veterinary professor shakes her head.

I think the starting point is contact with the real thing. Papier-mâché and varnish, parts that come apart or click into place, that's not what anyone's going to find when they cut open a body.

This was supposed to be Iris's discussion.

Why don't we . . . ?

They seem surprised that she's still there.

Why don't we continue this conversation in the veterinary gallery, she says, where we can see the horse itself?

And after that why don't we walk up to the park, adds the woman in glasses, and see a horse itself?

Everyone laughs except Iris. She leads the way and does not let herself look back. Raif and his friend take their time, the group has to wait, and when they arrive they walk through the door arm in arm. Iris can't think of anything to say. She stares at the horse.

The professor begins to point out certain aspects of the model and Iris moves away as if another object in the room needs her urgent attention. Some minutes later Raif comes over with the woman, whom he introduces as a colleague. Her name is Meike. She is in her thirties and almost too tall, her hair almost too heavy, to be beautiful. But she is beautiful. She has the profile of a wizard.

That was so interesting, says Meike. Thank you so much.

Iris has just understood. Her thick glasses, her loose gaze, the hand on Raif's arm.

You're blind!

Both Meike and Raif laugh, although he looks shocked.

Iris is shaking her head.

I'm sorry. I didn't mean—

That's OK.

Is it? Iris scrutinises Meike's laughing face. She can't tell.

I'm more like partially sighted. So a bit blind, yes. Quite a bit.

She puts her hand on Iris's arm and everything is alright.

In which case we can help, says Iris. I mean with the horse. Audio texts, high-resolution images, whatever you need, really, we'd be very happy to . . .

Raif thinks Iris is terribly upset. He doesn't know that she's not the type to dwell on minor catastrophes. She will mend what she can and move on. And she prefers to do something rather than talk about it and wants to stop talking right now. Meike interjects.

Is it possible to touch the horse?

It's the one thing that Iris can't help her with.

When I first came to work here you could. The horse had no case then. Come to think of it, we didn't use gloves either unless there was a known hazard.

Raif speaks without thinking.

Do you miss touch?

I don't know, she says. I'm used to using gloves and anyway we know now what damage we can do to things just by touching them.

Even lightly? asks Meike.

Iris pauses. She doesn't want to have this conversation with Meike. She wants to have it with Raif.

The slightest touch will leave a residue, she says. The surface may be compromised.

Raif echoes Iris so quietly that he might be whispering in her ear.

The slightest touch.

Either Meike hasn't picked up on the tension or she doesn't want to be left out. She has another point to make and turns to address the rest of the group.

Apparently we can't touch the horse. It's extremely fragile and its surfaces might be compromised.

It was a working model, Iris says. So it has withstood plenty of human contact. I mean, look – it's still intact, still functional after a hundred and fifty years.

The others look to Meike, who continues.

But it's obsolete. It's varnish and paper.

So does it teach us something about papier-mâché or the horse? says the professor.

Raif sees that Iris is distressed. He surprises himself by wanting to speak for her.

The model teaches us what this man at this time thought a horse was – which is just as important as what a horse is.

He is standing close to her, he is speaking for her, they are once again side by side.

When the group leaves, Iris stays behind. Raif walks Meike out but then comes back.

You were so kind, he says, and your talk, your talk was—

A disaster.

She realises that she's somehow made things awkward again and she gives way.

Look, she says with unnecessary firmness, do you want to have lunch?

Now?

No. Some other time.

He waits for her to say why. Is there something she'd like his advice on? Is there a project coming up to which he might contribute? But she doesn't. They stand there and smile at each other.

Yes, he says. That would be. Yes.

In the months since they first met, they've been brought together by chance and design. They've been wading out of themselves and towards one another despite all that has risen up or pulled them back. And now they've said, indirectly but out loud, that they want to meet and need no excuse to do so.

he wants to speak

Raif isn't tentative with Helen because he lacks the capacity to feel strongly. Perhaps just once we feel enough to erupt out of our constructions and offer our full selves. Raif wanted everything with Liis, believed everything, felt everything. How to recover?

And because he's never known how to answer the question people always ask – *Who are you?* – he has developed a habit of silence. Liis was someone whose reticence met his own. After she died his silence was no longer met and he understood that if he did not speak while someone was there – his father, his wife – he might never be able to do so. And there were things he needed to ask and to say.

Three months after Liis's death, Meike walked into his office and he felt a roaring in his body – something he'd known before his marriage, when he'd been less guarded and more determined about sex. This was another way in which he'd grown silent. He soon realised that Meike had this effect on everyone and that it provoked as much fear as desire. She drew everyone's gaze but because she did not return it, people felt that they'd never quite seen her.

He took her to the talk because she's working on nineteenth-century educational models. Also (but he did not know this) because he wanted Iris to see him at his most alive. He didn't realise that turning up with a beautiful unexplained woman might confuse the situation.

Having agreed with Iris that they will have lunch soon, he catches up with Meike at the station. They get on the same train, which is crowded and they have to stand. As ever Raif feels the roaring in his body (has it been caused by Iris?) and he works hard in the lurching carriage not to brush against her.

Well, isn't she exotic!

The man who says it is in his fifties, smartly dressed, staggering and red-faced. Raif turns to him.

At school he said nothing to the king of the boys. He said nothing to his mother and nothing to his wife. Now he wants to speak.

What did you say?

The man snorts. A couple of people laugh while others tut and shake their heads. The man prods his finger unsteadily in Meike's direction.

I said *isn't she exotic*. And who the fuck are you, anyway?

I'm the person who's going to tell you to apologise, Raif says.

He's still full of astonishment at the step he and Iris have just taken. Why did they wait months to say anything? All that talk about the merman and the cloud mirror, those messages about the weather, when it could just be said. *We want to meet*. Anything could – and should – be said!

Meike turns to face the man, who tries to step back.

Is she looking at me? Why's she looking at me?

Apologise, says Raif.

As the man burps and smirks and waggles his head, three teenage girls pull out their phones and take his picture.

There, one of them says. You're going to be famous.

What the fuck do you mean? says the man. You can't do that.

Do what?

They put their phones away but they keep staring – not at Meike, at him.

Other passengers have gathered courage now. Some are muttering about the man being a *disgrace* while others say *Leave him alone . . . He doesn't mean anything by it.* The lights in the carriage flicker as the train rasps and rattles on.

She's a witch! the man slurs. A fucking witch.

The teenagers brandish their phones again.

Care to repeat that? one of them says. You'll be really famous then.

She's not a witch, Raif says quietly. She's a wizard.

To Meike, the encounter with the drunk is routine. For Raif, it's momentous. He knows she doesn't need his help, let alone his protection, but he has spoken. It's a small thing. He's not what anyone in the carriage will remember but he believes he's found a way to say things and that people will listen.

The drunk has shut his eyes and seems about to fall asleep on his feet when a jolt brings him to and he sees that the annoying little man and the blind witch are still there.

Think this is my stop, he says to no one in particular.

Raif moves to stand between him and the doors.

Then you need to apologise.

He has not raised his voice but the man looks childishly down at the floor.

OK then, he says and turns to Meike, holding out his hand.

The lights flicker again. A few people giggle in response but most are focused on Meike. She reaches out her hand as if about to take his, only she doesn't. She lays her fingers on his wrist and slowly traces the length of his arm, her hand coming to rest on his shoulder. Raif has never seen anyone look more paralysed.

The lights flicker again and go out just as Meike pulls back her hand and slaps the man hard. Or does she? No one has seen. No one has a photograph.

space so easily overthrown

Up on the hill we can see right across the city and so locate ourselves outside it. We can follow two strangers coming towards each other as if we were telling a story. They are of no more significance than any other two among the millions and yet each step and gesture they make will be somehow familiar. They are not new to this and neither are we. We must recognise, through these strangers, what it means to repeat ourselves and we must decide whether repetition is a way forward or back.

Every year the towers grow taller, giving those permitted to enter them increasingly remote perspectives. Those who have no place in the towers can pay to visit, via a sealed lift, the top of the highest (or close to the top). If you rise to the seventy-second floor, the city will cease to make sense because at such a height all detail is lost. You will see brick, concrete, glass, steel and stone as texture rather than place.

Only the river becomes more clear. It is the one unbroken thing, strange and seemingly alive, indifferent to the city that lines its path. The river pulls in what light there is and passes through. The point is not to map the city but to find our way towards each other within it while the river runs on.

display

Iris proposed lunch so she leaves it to Raif to suggest where they might meet. He overhears a colleague talking about a pub that has log fires and good food and he looks it up and sends Iris the address. She's charmed because it's called The Blue Iris.

The daylight is like lamplight. Iris concentrates on finding the right tiny street among the rotting timbered facades, the efficient cafes, the quaint sex shops with their smudged cardboard signs, the side doors open onto anonymous stairs. When she arrives at The Blue Iris she's shown to a long mirrored room with clubbish armchairs set intimately around small tables. Raif is already there.

I'm so sorry, he says. This was a mistake. Do you mind?

Do I mind?

The place I meant to book is called The Blue Horse. Shall we find somewhere more . . . I don't know . . . not so . . .

Iris has picked up a menu.

They do nuts, crisps, cheese and ham. That's fine by me. Shall we get a drink?

He doesn't understand this unsmiling woman but evidently she can solve anything. As soon as they've sat down it seems wonderfully usual to be in this bar together on a weekday winter afternoon. Iris leans back in her chair, looking just right in her charcoal dress. It is more tailored than anything he's seen her in before (or perhaps he's only just allowed himself to take her in). She knows how to place herself and what to say. When the waiter comes over she orders for them both, making a technical adjustment to her drink.

Raif remembers the photo on her phone.

Are your children looking forward to Christmas?

I suppose so. It's difficult.

Oh?

Their father and I are no longer.

He waits for her to say no longer what but she doesn't.

I'm sorry, he says. That must be very sad.

I'm not sad.

But she is. She will never be happy in a complete way again.

What about you? Do you have children?

She sounds brisk, as if she's telling someone off.

Children? Sorry, no, I'm afraid not. No children. My wife died.

Other women to whom Raif has given this news have leant forward, taken his hand and gently prompted more detail. Iris takes a gulp of her drink and fixes her gaze on a corner of the ceiling.

Were you happy? You and your wife?

She's thinking of David, who might die too.

Raif is surprised into saying something that's never occurred to him before.

It made me happy to love her.

Iris looks at the corner of the ceiling again.

I did my best to love my husband.

But you didn't?

I believed I did. No, that's not true.

She tries to think of something more encouraging to say.

And did she love you, your wife?

He borrows his mother's explanation.

She was in shock.

This is something Iris can get hold of. She relaxes.

What do you mean?

He tells Iris the story of Liis in New York.

That was your wife? I read about her somewhere.

Iris hasn't asked how Liis died, which he thinks is a matter of delicacy whereas she isn't much interested. She wants to know about how the defection of Liis's father played out but Raif has no more details to offer and doesn't want to tell her that the story may be someone else's. They talk and drink, not noticing the bar fill up, the lights dim and the mood change. The waiter removes the vase of bright winter berries from their table and replaces it with a lantern. Music they hadn't noticed grows louder.

Iris talks about how many objects there are in the stores that have never been displayed.

I don't think an object is less important because it isn't seen.

What kind of thing is never displayed?

I suppose the ones that don't provide an answer or tell part of a story. And the ones that aren't valuable or rare or just don't look like anything.

Are you saying there are objects in your collections that are boring?

Not to me but yes. There are things that are too shocking to be seen as well.

So what constitutes boring?

A broken stick? Sixteenth-century and the standard measurement here for a couple of hundred years but to families on a day out and tourists on an itinerary, it's a broken stick.

Raif tries once again to take a step towards her.

Would you rather be shocking or boring?

He is being playful but to Iris this is a serious question and she gives it thorough consideration.

I'd like to look boring but have a shocking history.

Is that who she is? He thinks it might be.

The music is turned up once more and a nearby couple start to dance. They barely move but dancing gives them permission to lean fully into one another. Their bodies tilt, so slowly, to one side and then the other. And then the music lurches and the woman throws back her head and the man presses his mouth to her throat. Then they open their eyes and remember where they are. Raif and Iris watch them.

a yardstick

Everything used to be measured according to ourselves. There was the hand, the foot and also the yard, which was (among other things) the distance from the king's nose to the tip of his outstretched thumb. (But which king?)

The museum possesses instruments designed to measure criminals' skulls, the barrel of a gun, the earth's density, the brain's activity, the breath, the truth. All depend on a constant. Queen Elizabeth I had this particular yardstick made of bronze as the standard for the nation. It was the measure of all measures for almost two centuries.

As people travelled the world, they met other forms of measurement. They needed a constant that could accompany them on their travels. A committee was formed which decided that this international constant would be a measurement that could be multiplied up to the full extent of the earth and so applied to any extent – a ten millionth of a quarter of a circle around the earth. It took six years, at a time of great sickness and war, to measure the designated distance and to define what was called the metre, and which was more or less the distance from a king's nose to the tip of his outstretched thumb.

The standard *mètre des Archives* was cast in platinum in 1799 but through the next century of enlightenment and revolution, uncertainty grew. People were looking more closely now, naming the elements and exposing their instabilities. In the great compromise of 1889, a series of standards were cast in a platinum-iridium alloy, one of which took the place of the *mètre des Archives*, and one of which was received by Britain.

But how could the modern world measure itself by a single metal bar? People searched once more for a natural constant that did not have to be compared or cast and, a hundred years after the platinum-iridium bar, settled upon the speed of light. And here we are, the structure of light breaking down and its constancy in question.

rain

Iris is offered a last-minute place at a conference in Paris because one of her colleagues has fallen ill. She accepts. Travel weakens us so that memories, especially sense memories, can be overwhelming. If you're in a foreign city, in a place that's hard to take in, listening to a language you don't speak, and you suddenly encounter the scent or detail of someone you absolutely know, it can be shocking.

She is woken by rain. She's in a room under the eaves in a university block and the sound returns her to an attic room where she slept with a man for whom she left a life. Beyond that lies the room they ran away to, where they made love in the dark during an electrical storm. The lightning photographed certain moments she can still see.

The rain reaches her before she wakes so that by the time she does wake, she's already in pain. The grief of that other man's absence is real and new. Iris has to walk all day to get past it and during that time she feels nothing for Raif, nothing for David, nothing for her daughters. She walks until she feels nothing at all.

a small green space

The city is full of trees, reinforcing the idea that it's not a city at all but a series of villages. Who can feel they belong in a place that is almost a thousand square miles? It breaks down out of necessity. You are not in the city but in a district or street. You can't see everything at once or keep all you know in mind, just as you can't arrange to meet someone in the city. You have to contrive a smaller place.

When Iris tells the story of this love she likes to make clear that they ran away together and that this caused someone else great pain. It is how she makes sense of what she allowed him to do to her. She met Adam when she spent the summer after graduation working with a team assessing a town hall for conservation while it was being prepared for sale. The team took note of every original feature: the skirtings, escutcheons, bathroom tiles and drawer handles. Iris couldn't tell what was original or not. Something was identified and she went round the building recording it. She had already decided that she wanted to be a conservator and had a place to study for a masters degree that autumn.

A shop opposite the town hall was being refitted and one day she passed the open door and saw a man building a spiral staircase. Had he been building anything else – a cupboard, shelves, plain stairs – she would not have lingered. But a spiral staircase! He was not only a carpenter but a mathematician and artist as well!

Adam was huge and he shaved his head so that his face, which looked as if it had been hewn from stone, was all the more fierce. When he spoke he sounded Danish, South African, Irish . . . It turned out that he'd lived in all those places.

It was a brief time of golden evenings and when Iris finished work she didn't hurry back to her studio flat. She took to sitting in a disused Quaker cemetery filled by an ancient capsized fig. The cemetery's low brick walls leant against the offices that had grown up around it. It was one of those small green spaces to be found all over the city, where people think themselves unobserved, especially on golden evenings. You will see them, lovers in office clothes who have waited all day to hold hands and who must soon go home, only for now there is a small space in which what they do doesn't count and isn't wrong. It's such a small space. Why do you think they look so sad?

One evening Adam appeared (had she mentioned the cemetery?) and sat down beside her. They talked a bit and then she set off home. The next day Iris went there again and so did he. After a week of this, Adam took her hand and told her that he was about to get married. He kept hold of her hand, something she couldn't reconcile with what he was saying. From that point on, she failed to connect their conversations with what lay beyond them. (Failed or refused?)

Iris felt as if she were climbing a spiral staircase, finding the hidden perfected shape of things and even of herself.

She also thought herself immune, so much so that she asked him about the woman he was engaged to.

How did you meet her?

I'm a journeyman. I set out on a journey.

You mean after your apprenticeship?

That's right. I had five coins in my pocket and was forbidden to go home for three years.

When is your time up?

Adam shrugged. Two years ago, maybe?

A man who could build a spiral staircase and travel the world with five coins in his pocket. Only Adam didn't seem like someone with only five coins. His work clothes, his bag and boots looked expensive. Iris would not let herself ask where he was living, how long he'd been in the city or where he was going next.

How did you meet her?

He'd got talking to her father on a train in Ireland, helped him into a taxi, shared the ride and after being directed towards a place where he could pitch his tent, returned to the old man's cottage. He was a retired teacher and he liked to talk. They drank whisky till midnight.

I set off back down the hill and when I turned to call out goodnight, I saw a light on and someone at an attic window.

The princess in the tower?

Precisely.

The next day Adam walked up to the cottage again and there was a woman in the front garden hanging sheets on a line.

I introduced myself and she just nodded. I explained

that I was there to repay the old man's hospitality, that I could rehang the gate or mend the fence. Was he her father, I asked, and she nodded again and gestured towards the house.

She was dumb?

She didn't speak.

Beautiful?

Iris despised herself for asking this and was not pleased by his answer.

Dark, wild hair, furious-looking.

Clever?

In a way. I stayed for the rest of the summer and—

That was that?

He ran a finger across Iris's mouth.

That was that.

The stranger on the train, the light in the window, the silent princess. It was a story that required an absolute gesture. Of course he'd proposed to her.

One evening Adam told Iris that his work on the shop had ended. She thought she was relieved. It was a chance to conclude whatever this was without harm. Iris was the one who wrote down her number and address. The shop opened and she went in on its first day. The spiral staircase led nowhere and was used to display shoes. She was unsettled by the extent of her distress.

You can say yes without knowing that you've done so. Late one night Iris's doorbell rang. Adam was standing there surrounded by plastic bags. Iris suggested that they carry them up to her flat, to get them out of her neighbours' way, and he seemed to take this as her agreeing to a proposition he hadn't yet mentioned. The bags were thin and carelessly filled and as she and Adam hauled them up the three flights they left a trail of his possessions. When she turned to go back for them he shook his head and shut the door. The first time he sat down in her one armchair he looked at home. From that moment Iris felt a responsibility to meet his conviction with her own.

They went to bed, where he dedicated himself to her pleasure. Her body felt nothing. For that one night she wondered if she was making a terrible mistake but by the morning she was in love. He still hadn't explained what brought him to her with all his bags. In the end she asked.

I told her the marriage was a mistake. So I had to leave right away.

Leave where?

We've been staying at her aunt's place.

Every evening after they'd left the cemetery he'd gone home to the princess. Of course he had. They were getting married. It took several days for Iris to gather the courage to ask more.

When you told her you were leaving, what did she say? Sorry, I forgot that she doesn't speak.

Iris had imagined a language of gestures.

Of course she can speak. But she has a terrible stutter.

The silent princess.

Is that why she still lived with her father?

With her father? She worked in Cork, in IT. Most of the time he's left to fend for himself in that breeze-block bungalow.

The cottage on the hill. The light in the high window.

They kept finding things for me to do. The fence, the window frames, the doors. By the end I'd more or less rebuilt the place. Everything fitted beautifully.

Why did you leave?

When I've finished the work, I move on.

A letter arrived. The princess wanted Iris to know that she had left a job and her dying father to come to be married. That her aunt could not keep her. She asked Iris to give him up. (Had she taken him?) The letter was on the table in front of him but he made no attempt to read it.

Questions swelled in Iris's chest but she could only voice the smallest.

How did she get hold of my address?

I gave it to her.

When Iris read the letter from the princess, with its childish phrasing, spelling errors and raw threats, she felt nothing. Her life had been smashed into and she was stunned.

the real thing

While they were still fizzy with new love, Adam took Iris to visit a friend he described as a mystic novelist.

What does that mean? What kind of books does she write?

Nothing conventional.

Are they about love and how to live?

On the highest level, yes.

Perhaps I've read something. Which is your favourite?

I don't know. All of them.

You've read all her books? How many are there?

So many I can't remember.

The train passed painted cottages and run-down farms, any of which could be where a novelist lived, but the station they got off at was next to an industrial park. They followed a track round the edge of a housing development that led to a row of wartime prefabs built of corrugated iron. One had windowsills lined with animal skulls, another a wooden boat leaning against the wall, a gash in its hull. There was a garden full of withered cacti in red plastic pots.

Artists live here, Adam said.

The place made Iris sad.

Tina was in her garden, painting. She was very thin and wore old beige cashmere and a long necklace of roughly polished stones. Just like a romantic novelist, Iris planned to tease Adam later. She didn't know yet that he was not to be teased.

Tina's house was as tightly organised and equipped as the cabin of someone embarking on a long voyage. She took her time showing them all that she had accomplished. It seemed that she did everything – wrote her books, painted everything, made everything, grew everything. When she offered tea she poured some of the leaves into her hand and commanded Adam to smell them. *Rose pouchong!* Iris stored this away as a joke, noting exactly how she said it.

After tea Tina proposed a walk by the river. The water was slow and brown, and the land around it one of those pockets of dullness that the countryside throws up, but Tina entered the scene as if she'd walked into a painting. She kept pointing things out to Adam, her arm through his.

Look, Adam, a kingfisher! Do you think that's a trout pool, Adam? Look!

He delighted in whatever she conjured and didn't once turn to share his delight with Iris. She trailed behind them for a while and when they didn't seem to notice, inserted herself between them like a jealous child. They walked on in silence. There were no more kingfishers or trout pools.

Do you remember our trip to the bank, Adam? Tina said.

Of course. You were magnificent!

We found some money, she explained to Iris. It was just lying there on the street. Toy money, I mean.

And it was right outside a bank, said Adam, so guess what Tina did?

Iris refused to guess so Tina explained.

I tried to bank it.

What about the cashier? Iris asked.

He was at a loss. Totally. Wasn't he, Adam? Poor boy.

Perhaps he didn't get the joke? Iris knew she sounded unnecessarily upset.

It wasn't a joke, Tina said.

Adam explained.

Tina likes to test procedures. It's part of her practice.

This didn't sound like him, or what Iris knew of him, at all.

As they were leaving, Tina embraced Iris and said that she was sorry the two of them hadn't had the chance to talk more. She hadn't asked Iris a single question all afternoon. On the train home Adam was quiet. He asked if Iris had a headache. She said she did.

Iris and Adam were still in bright light. When something troubling arose she took note but put it away so quickly that she could tell herself that she hadn't heard or seen. She was stepping behind walls of her own making.

A year later she was in the middle of an argument with Adam when that day rose up in her mind and at last she was able to speak of how miserable she'd been. Adam was amazed.

But I was so happy! he said.

Because you were with Tina!

No. You. I was happy because I was in love with you.

But you were completely wrapped up in each other. *Look, Adam!* Remember? The fucking trout pool or whatever it was in that muddy little river. You were so curious, so enthusiastic, and I was left behind!

I was showing you that I was in love!

It took several more years for Iris to see how this made sense. In walking beside Tina, and looking with her, Adam had been performing his delight in his love. And Iris would come to admire people like Tina and how she invested all she did. Her ecstatic approach to the world was sincere. And perhaps Tina hadn't been rude. She just couldn't be bothered with the etiquette of being interested in or including Iris.

Adam had several answers for every question.

Perhaps he's just more truthful, Iris said to her friends.

She was about to give up her flat and her course to travel with Adam. It would be a year before she saw any of these friends again.

He arrived in my life as if that's where he was always meant to be.

Everyone thinks that.

About everyone.

What makes him so special?

Iris tried to sound as if she knew.

She was someone who measured everything. Men had taken their cue from her and approached tentatively. They had circled her, whereas Adam surrounded her. He hadn't approached at all. He was just there. The joy she then experienced, despite all she observed in him, was that of release. She had never felt so held.

Such love lifts you beyond the clouds and you lose all sense of direction and scale. You come to need the pull of the earth. Iris and Adam lurched from place to place, chasing jobs, alienating friends and scrabbling for money while his certainty rolled out before everything like a long smooth road. And then his certainty wasn't enough. She no longer recognised herself. They were living in Spain, in a mountain hut, when Iris's mother forwarded a letter asking her to confirm her return to the course. When Iris raised this with Adam he disappeared for twenty-four hours. Once the deadline had passed, Iris mentioned the course again. This time Adam just shrugged.

If that's what you want to do.

But I can't. It's too late.

For a while he was sweet and contented. He had set her a test and by not replying to the letter she'd passed it. But Iris liked things to be complete. She wondered, out loud, if she was ever going to finish the course and Adam punched her in the face. She saw him hesitate for a moment, not in an attempt to control himself but while making the decision to do it. He punched her in the face and then he walked out.

Iris did nothing to stop him leaving. She couldn't because she wasn't there. She was ten years old, sitting on the sofa with her brother Jason, listening to her mother explain that her father had gone.

Why? asked Jason.

Because I don't want him.

Doesn't he want me?

Iris had said nothing. She knew, from her bad dreams, that there were silences which were part of being a family. You didn't ask such questions because life depended on some things never being put into words. She met walls and so built her own because the worst thing could happen and it had. Her father had gone.

And because he never came back, Iris, alone in the night in a hut on a mountain, assumed Adam wouldn't either. So when he appeared an hour later and went to elaborate lengths to fashion a cold compress for her face out of a tea towel and a bowl of snow, she was amazed and grateful. She felt as much joy as she would have had her father come home.

She pleaded with Adam to hold her and when he lay down and put a single limp arm across her body she pleaded some more. She needed to feel that she was back inside the small green space of his certainty. What could she do?

Do something, she said. Whatever you want.

What he wanted hurt and he knew it and so he forgave her.

It took her another six months to leave him. When she told him she'd written to the college, he pushed her out of the car and left her on the side of the road. She walked back to the hut and they had a fight during which her arm was broken. She was never sure exactly how it happened. The kindness of the doctors was the shock that made her realise how little she'd come to expect. While Adam fussed over her in hospital, and the nurses remarked on his devotion, Iris said nothing. *I am nothing*, she thought. *I have no home, money, work or friends. I live with a man I believe could kill me and I behave accordingly.* Adam brought in her passport for the hospital paperwork. The doctor let her ring her mother, who hadn't heard from her for a year but asked no questions and arranged a flight home. Iris never saw Adam again.

The panic attacks started one day when she was on the underground. The train braked hard and when the man standing beside her stumbled and raised his arm to grab at the strap, she crumpled to the floor as if she'd been punched in the face. The man was big like Adam and the carriage about the size of the mountain hut. The echo of a gesture struck her so forcefully that she felt afterwards that she was full of cracks, like a piece of stone which, hit by lightning, reveals its strata having never been solid at all.

When Iris was about to marry David, Adam inhabited her dreams. She woke each morning in terrible pain which she realised was self-disgust. She did not recognise the person who had gone on pulling towards such a man, pleading with him to stay.

You were young, said her friends, the night before the wedding.

But that suggests I was some other self who can be discounted now I've come to my senses. Only I am that person. I will always be that person.

Iris and Adam strode the earth as if they were the manifestation of something other people could only aspire to. She would never believe in anything on that scale again.

This is who I am, thought Iris as she travelled towards David the next morning. *Someone capable of letting a man step into my life and take control – even of what I feel and think. I turned away from what he was stepping out of and what he might bring.* Perhaps the pattern was being repeated? After all, David had surrounded her too. Only this time there was no danger. She had by then surrounded herself.

shall I leave you now?

Neither Iris nor Raif would say that they are in love but they have turned towards one another.

He invites her to meet some of his colleagues to discuss her possible involvement in a debate about the conservation of objects. It's the last week of term and the group move on to a nearby pub. Raif's head of department arrives and sits down beside them.

So, Raif, she says, this debate you're organising will pitch conservation against digital archive?

It was the students' idea. They want to argue for and against the letting go of objects. Rather than trying to salvage or preserve them to the extent that they are no longer themselves.

And whose side are you on? She is addressing Iris.

She's mine, says Raif.

He sounds matter-of-fact but his meaning flares.

The objects, says Iris. I'm on the side of the objects. That's why I'm here. To discuss the debate.

Raif and Iris don't need to look at, or even speak to, one another. They both have that feeling of being side by side. They think it's safe to enjoy their connection in this silent way. Nothing has happened, no one can see anything. Or can they?

Oh, says the woman. I thought when he said you were his, he meant that you are together. That you are a couple.

She is so blunt and inexpressive that Iris can detect no mischief. But who would say such a thing out loud? Were she and Raif about to say what they thought too? That he had been deliberately ambiguous and it had delighted her?

No, says Iris, who cannot control her smile. Not that. No. The woman is neither perturbed by her mistake nor particularly interested. She had cast about for conversation with a stranger and there it had been. She talks a little more to Iris about her work at the museum and then turns to someone else.

Iris says she should be going and Raif takes her up to his office, where she left her bag. They are talking – about what? – when his hand reaches out and touches her cheek as if testing the surface of something extremely frail. She will remember how solemn he looks as he does this and how she feels herself take on the same gravity.

They have stepped aside into another dimension where he reaches out past grief and loss and touches her. In that other place she hears herself asking *Shall I leave you now?* And him saying *Yes*.

the towers

There is a day in early December when snow falls but so lightly that it's gone before it reaches the ground. Scribbles form and melt all the dark afternoon.

When David phones and asks if he can come round to talk, Iris is surprised to find that she's relieved. The last year falls away, Raif with it, as they settle down with a bottle of wine. It's as if he never left and had no reason to and she knows what he's going to say.

I can't do it, he begins.

Iris feels as if she's taking up the ground from beneath her feet but she makes herself say it.

You can come back.

David looks calm but he is starting to cry.

I can't, he says. I can't.

Iris is shaking her head. She doesn't understand. He tries to explain.

I did what you asked. I left. And I've been here for the girls. Have you ever thought what it's like for me coming back twice a week, into what was my home, being with my children and then having to leave again?

For her, he is simply there or not there. She hasn't dared imagine what the hours of his days are like, let alone his nights. Why has it not occurred to her that being placed outside your life might have its own effect? She thinks of her mother placing her father outside their life and how she has done this to her husband too. Only David has done things to place himself outside. Perhaps that's why he did them. They are both crying now. David has never found it so difficult to speak.

I can see now that I haven't got . . . we haven't got . . . we can't . . . there's been too much . . .

She sits back and considers him. He looks sad but determined, brave even. Perhaps he always has been but the hundred Davids who have disappointed or enraged her have stood in the way. *I did love him*, she thinks as all the Irises who have obstructed her heart step back.

At last it has come to an ending. They sit there in silence. They do not need to speak of anything more right now.

The city rises up around them. It has been described as a place through which we move – travelling towards, away from or past one another. Even endings are moved through as if they were punctuation rather than conclusion. But the city is also a place of arrest. We have to negotiate its traffic and its architecture as well as each other. And there are always too many of us, moving too slowly, encumbered, perhaps lost.

An ending is built after the fact, just like a beginning. It can take years. Detail has to pass into memory, feeling into story, so that what we recall is brightly painted, sturdily constructed, accessible, predictable and satisfactory. We can point to it from far away and others can see it clearly. Like the tallest towers in the city, from a certain distance our beginnings and endings are all that can be seen.

the heart

The museum has acquired a state-of-the-art cardiac-patient simulator. This is a dummy moulded onto a resuscitation bed, the body reduced to site. His face is convincing, he's even got hair. You can take his pulse in his wrist and his breath can be expressed in six different sounds but otherwise he's reduced to the parts on which the doctors will focus. He ends at the hips and his groin is smooth.

This heart is designed to be probed, wired, recorded and shocked. It can present with ten standardised scenarios and fifty different conditions including high or low pressure and a variety of blockages and troubling rhythms.

We rely on the continuous onward momentum of the heart and want above all not to notice it. If we do, we believe it to be precarious. We don't think of it as its true brute self but as a flutter, a patter. It can also pound and ache, jump, leap, cry out or bleed. It can be heavy, cold or sore, warm, full or broken. A heart can be left somewhere or given away. It can be gold, stone or ice; pure, empty or open. Perhaps because it is so invested, we can only think of it as a simple shape. We see hearts everywhere and seek them out. We share pictures of heart-shaped pebbles, petals, cupcakes and sunglasses. Clouds, forests, fireworks and lakes appear heart-shaped. We point at them and say *Look, a heart!*

Raif's heart is a series of small consolations. Iris's

heart, so tightly layered, is no more easily navigable. The cartoon shape is the one we find easiest to grasp and remember. It is not, on the whole, a reflection of the way we feel.

glare

David takes the girls to his parents for Christmas. This seems right to Iris. It's what they're used to and enjoy. She tells them brightly that she'll spend the day with friends and has prepared more detail, only they don't ask for it. They want to know that she'll be alright but no more than that or they might not be able to believe her.

Iris has had several invitations but the prospect of inserting herself into other people's Christmases or proving herself good value exhausts her. So she tells her friends she's going home to her mother and her mother that she'll be with friends. On the day she's restless. She's enjoying the space that she's contrived but does not know how to fill it.

Where is Raif? For the first time she wonders what he's doing at a particular moment. She decides that he is with his mother at a large and otherwise empty table. The badly cooked food is almost untouched. His mother tries to start a conversation but he doesn't respond because he can't stop thinking about Iris. Any minute now he'll leave the table and go into the garden to call to wish her Happy Christmas and then, when he discovers she's alone, he'll jump into his car and drive back to the city and they'll spend the rest of the day in bed, spilling champagne on the sheets and undoing delightful parcels wrapped in tissue paper and tied with ribbons.

Christ. She knows so little about him that this is all her mind can come up with. But it's what she wants. Someone who will travel towards her with such momentum and certainty that she can do nothing to resist. The moment he reached out and touched her face felt as powerful as if he'd driven a hundred miles to declare his love. Why did she ask if she should leave and why did he say yes?

Her phone doesn't ring. By early afternoon she needs to escape this waiting and so drives out of the city. She stops at a service station. They're serving a Christmas special and she takes it, saying to the man behind the counter that she'll be eating another Christmas meal tonight *when I get there*. She is trying to appear on her way somewhere. She even makes herself hurry.

Raif's mother assumes he will join her for Christmas and he does not contradict her. He tells Helen that this is an obligation and he's sure she wants to see her family too, so why don't they have a meal on Christmas Eve? Rosa is back for a week, and she and her partner will be joining them as well as a couple of Spanish actors Helen's been working with.

Why not come on Christmas Eve? his mother asks. Sorcha and Neil will drop in for a bite before midnight mass, the triplets too.

I'm just—

Too sad, his mother assumes. Even though it's now more than two years since Liis died, she explains Raif to herself in terms of grief. He hasn't yet mentioned Helen.

Christmas Eve is convivial. Everyone brings a dish they grew up with and they all tell stories and Raif feels as happy as he does when the triplets come to stay. Like then his home is full of life that requires no effort to sustain it. They eat devils on horseback, almond soup, paella, curry and roti, and bûche de Noël. Raif relishes it all but he's not thinking, as Helen is, that this is their first Christmas together and what that might mean.

Rosa pulls out her phone to photograph the food.

Who made the devils on angels, these things, whatever they're called? You, Raif? Line up.

She wants everyone standing beside their dish and takes pictures of them all. One of the actors asks for a picture of his hosts and the other goes to get Helen from the kitchen.

A photo of the lovely couple, please! A souvenir! The lovely couple!

Helen lets them move her into position next to Raif, beside a pretty Japanese screen that is hers and just as their guests raise their phones to picture the lovely couple, Raif steps behind the screen. They pause.

What are you doing, Raif?

Everyone can hear Helen's desperation.

It's a joke! he says but doesn't step back.

Rosa moves quickly to stand beside Helen.

We are the lovelier couple, surely!

And they all laugh and take a picture and the moment passes.

On Christmas morning Raif and Helen exchange presents and go for a walk.

That was a lovely evening, she says. Our friends got on so well.

The food was delicious but there's so much left over.

It was sweet of Alberto to want a photo of us.

Was it? I thought he was just being polite. I mean, we barely know them.

I've been working with them for weeks. We're friends.

You hadn't mentioned them before.

I had. You just don't—

Is she going to say it? And is she then going to press him about his *joke*? That moment will remain with Helen forever because when she stepped into place beside Raif and faced the smiling room she had thought *At last*. But today she says nothing and when her brother arrives to pick her up she tells him what a great evening they had and asks Raif to give his mother her love. She's lent him her car to drive down there.

Raif watches a film and picks at leftovers, putting off leaving even though he knows his mother is alone. He's told her he is keeping a colleague company, someone in the city without family, and will arrive mid-afternoon. They always have their Christmas meal in the early evening anyway.

He drives west towards the sun. Its heart, so absent and so intense, touches him. As the sun drops and deepens, the horizon rises in a blazing line. What must those passing make of this man who swerved off the road into a lay-by and is standing there in his shirtsleeves on this freezing day, taking picture after picture of an ordinary sky? And if they could see that he's weeping, would they understand?

where are you where I am?

Watch Iris and Raif as, over the weeks of midwinter, they leave for work and return home in the dark. Absorbed by the idea of each other, they notice the city only as backdrop. The streets are mysterious. Glimpses of towers and spires, sun and moon, punctuate the drama they now inhabit. They do not think about how many rooms are empty, those who have no room, and all the doors that are closed.

They meet by the river to discuss the forthcoming debate and decide that as it is a rare bright day, they should walk. They are their most graceful selves – measured, solemn and delighting. The detail of what has passed between them already seems so rich. It's as if they're being spun into something. Anything can be spun out of so much water and light. They pause on a bridge and lean over the rail, shoulder to shoulder, staring pointlessly at the water. The sun swivels its low beam to blind them and they only feel more.

They're walking off the bridge in that lemony light, almost holding hands, when Raif's phone rings. He's baffled – his phone never rings – and then pleased because it will seem to Iris that it often does. *Hello!* he says too cheerfully and then *Hello*, less certainly, and *Oh god* and *I see* and *Of course* and *How* and *When*.

Iris stands beside him watching the day contract into someone receiving terrible news. When the call ends he stands there looking past her. It's a while before he can speak.

He was my friend. I hadn't seen him for years. I had no idea.

Well, I'm your friend, she says, taking his hand. What can I do?

The man who has died was a cultural historian who'd been a friend of Raif's father's. The grief Raif now feels is out of all proportion to their connection and has to do with many things. The historian had encouraged Raif's interests and guided him towards his career, but they'd met only occasionally and hadn't stayed in touch.

Iris is the person who is there, holding his hand. She will help him through this. She mentions that she also knew the historian (he'd taught a course during her degree) and that they'd met at the museum once or twice. She asks if Raif would like her to come with him to the funeral. He does not say no.

On the day, Iris is late. Her card is rejected at the station so she walks to a cash machine that's not working. She decides to drive, which shouldn't take long but there are roadworks and diversions and every light hits red. There's a truck of scaffolding being unloaded, a medical emergency, a police cordon, wavering cyclists and dustbin lorries. All this she turns, as it's happening, into a story she will tell Raif. *I was late*, she will say, and then regale him with the comic detail of her calamitous journey and he will be grateful for her determination to be there to support him. He will take her hand.

As she gets near the crematorium she tries to follow the map on her phone but it keeps freezing and readjusting and is slow to give street names. Not that there are many signs. How could she have lived for so long in the city and have no idea how to navigate this part of it?

The funeral has begun and the crematorium is full so she finds a place at the back. She cannot help but look for Raif and there he is. When they stand, Iris remembers his grief and wants to move forward and let him know she's there but at that moment the woman beside him leans against him and he leans back. Iris watches. *She could be your sister. I don't even know if you have a sister. If she's a friend, is she a friend like me? Someone you fall into place with from time to time? Do you stand side by side in rooms? Does it feel special? Do you approach one another as if about to share a secret? Do you fuck?*

At this point she stops herself. This is someone's funeral and she isn't even there to mourn. What made her think Raif needed her? Afterwards she tries to leave as quickly as possible but bumps into someone she knows and when she's free to leave again, Raif appears. The woman is beside him and he introduces them. It is of course Helen, although Iris has been refusing to recognise her. She has that bouncy hair pinned up and anyway why would Iris remember her? Helen starts to say that they've met before when Iris interrupts.

I was late.

She says it because those are the words that have been kept waiting on the tip of her tongue.

Helen ignores this and asks how Iris knew the historian. She exaggerates their connection so as to explain her presence and then she wants to go.

My husband is taking care of the girls but I can't leave him alone with them too long. He has MS, you see.

Helen softens.

Your husband? I'm so sorry. That's awful.

She doesn't notice the jolt that passes through Raif. Later she will say how awful it must be for that poor woman to be coping with two children and a husband with MS. Raif will say nothing.

It is what it is, says Iris. Lovely to see you both.

She hurries away.

Someone comes into view and everything around them recedes. You have to isolate them like this in order to see them clearly. It's part of the enchantment and only when their life steps forward do you remember where this is taking place – in two as yet separate lives. Iris and Raif are such a small part of each other's lives. Now they will start to ask not only *Where are you?* but *Where are you where I am?*

Iris wakes, burning, at three a.m. She'd thought she was being brave, trusting the bond between them, and that her being at the funeral would mean something to him. Had he said he wanted her to come? He was just too polite to say no. Why had she thought he needed her? They hardly knew one another.

He'd never said he had a girlfriend. All he'd said was

that his wife was dead. So the girlfriend couldn't be that important but why had he not made things clear? Why was nobody ever clear?

She wakes an hour later and says aloud that she used a funeral as a place to meet Raif, and David's illness as a shield. And Raif was not who she thought he was. He'd made a fool of her. Liar. Fucking liar.

She wakes again. They've met a handful of times and have barely begun to talk about their lives. She gave the impression that her situation is less complicated than it really is. He did the same. It was only human.

She wakes again. This thing felt so good, so clean, but they were building it out of concealments and evasions and other people's pain. She remembers how Helen stood beside him. She remembers Adam, the fig tree and the Irish princess.

She wakes again.

a diversion from a conclusion

Raif is passing Helen in the hallway of the flat when he pulls her into an embrace.

I'm ready now, he says. You do understand, don't you?

Of course.

(Does she?)

It's almost two years and I've been meaning to . . . I keep thinking I should . . .

Should what?

Take her back. Her ashes. They're still here, you see, over there.

Helen has discovered Liis's ashes already but hasn't said so. She's tried to respect the fact of them, there on the shelf, still in the ugly tube the crematorium supplied. She's glad Raif wants to take them away.

To Estonia? That sounds like a good idea. I could come with you.

No. Thank you but—

I can look up flights, hotels, that kind of thing. When are you thinking of going?

As soon as I can.

He holds Helen more tightly.

It's been really hard to think about and now I need to get it done. You do understand, don't you?

She's kind enough to say yes and so he spends an hour making arrangements and another hour at his desk waiting for her to go to sleep. He answers every outstanding message and three times starts to write to Iris but stops himself. After all, their flirtation has already gone too far. When Iris and Helen were standing there together after the funeral he'd felt exposed, which meant that there was something to hide. He'd stood there looking from one to the other, realising that he hadn't thought of either of them as entirely real. Nor had he thought what he was doing with Iris (a couple of meetings, a lunch, a few messages) applied in any way to his life with Helen. Of course it did. He just hadn't thought.

Raif tells himself that he needs to commit properly to Helen and the first step in this is to conclude Liis's death. And Helen understands. He can see now that the weight on his chest is not the old pain of his marriage but guilt. He's a good man. He will not write to Iris.

So Raif puts Iris back beside her husband and children, and travels to Estonia, where he makes his way to the sea. This is the conclusion that he now seems to want so urgently but he's taken aback by the shallow scurrying water and can't bring himself to hold the ashes in his hands. In the end he opens the cardboard tube and trails it behind him as he walks along the edge of the water imagining a silver stream. His feet grow wet and he welcomes the cold when it comes and walks further than he has to before trying to sink the tube. In the end he just lets it go.

He walks until he finds a friendly-looking bar and there

is a woman in a silver coat. When he gets back to London they start to send messages.

Thank you for the photo of you in your silver coat. You look very beautiful. Here's one of me.

The picture he sends her is striking. With the sun behind him, he is almost in silhouette. It was taken by Helen soon after they started seeing each other.

Since coming back from Estonia he is preoccupied. Helen assumes he's thinking about Liis so says nothing. He's thinking, most of the time, about the woman in the silver coat. He sits in the same room as Helen sending and receiving messages as if to prove to himself that there's nothing wrong with this.

Thank you for your picture, shadow man, but I'm not sure I can see you. You are a mystery. I will be in London in April and I will bring my silver coat.

My life is a mystery even to me. I would like to meet you in April when the cherry blossom unfurls.

Unfurls? You are a poet, no?

I am not a poet. I am a shadow.

He tells her now that writing to her makes him happy because really he is so sad.

Shadow man, why so sad?

Because I have a broken heart.

At night he doesn't look at the photo of the woman in the silver coat but at one of Meike. It is of a group at a dinner, including him. He zooms in on her hand, which is raised just in front of her cleavage. She is holding a strawberry dipped in cream. After a moment he zooms out again. This happens deep in a dream. He does not know what he is doing – as much as anyone can not know such things.

He loses his phone often and one day finds that Iris has called three times in an afternoon without leaving a message. He makes a note to call her back.

There are many things of which he is ashamed: that he hasn't published another book and so has neither sought nor been offered promotion, that he never corrects people who mispronounce his name, that he did not insist to Liis on meeting her family, that he never asked her what he most wanted to, that he finds Helen both onerous and vital, and that he enjoys the numbness he feels and takes the pills he's been given in the hope that it will increase.

this is all true

It is out of what we do not know and cannot say that we take shape.

Raif wept by the side of the road on Christmas Day because he couldn't take a good enough picture of the setting sun. He met Iris in the New Year to draw her out about what position she might take in the debate. He lost an old friend and went to his funeral, which reminded him that he had to do something about Liis's ashes. He scattered them in the sea and then got drunk and poured his heart out to a stranger in a bar because there was nothing else to do. He came home to Helen.

This is all true. It is what's happened and how Raif would explain himself. It would surprise him to know that he's writing to the woman in the silver coat to stop himself writing to Iris. Or that he took his wife's ashes to Estonia to prove to his mother (whose end he can glimpse now) that he has learnt how to manage the dead. Or that he went to the historian's funeral convinced that by entering his father's past, he would be able to summon him. And he has turned towards Helen so as to have somewhere to put feelings that he isn't yet ready to understand. And because he is starting to feel close to her.

love

David is running towards his daughters when everything stops. They are standing at the top of the hill shouting at him to come and see – what? He'll never know because at that moment he contracts within his body and loses all force and reach. The hill rocks and then swallows him.

When he wakes up he knows where he is and who he is. He starts to get out of bed, only they still have him plugged into the machines. He doesn't struggle. He understands perfectly. He smiles at the person in the next bed, who doesn't respond, probably because he – or she – is so far away.

A young man leans over him.

How are you feeling? he asks.

David loves his mouth.

Like Gulliver! he says and the stranger smiles.

David loves him.

He must have fallen asleep. The machines have gone. There are people sitting beside his neighbour's bed and a child playing on the floor. A woman comes to help David sit up but he doesn't need her, he's fine.

On another day, or is it the same day, the woman sits beside him, shows him pictures and asks him lots of questions. David stares at the pictures because she keeps pointing. He nods and when she asks says no, he doesn't feel unwell, just very tired. While they are talking he starts to need something. He needs it more and more and so he stands up. There is a great pressure but he knows what to do. His hands find his penis. Where to put it? He sees a white bowl on the wall across the room and knows that this is what he's looking for and so he walks over, being careful not to step on the child, and relieves the pressure in a yellow stream. When he sits back down on his bed, the woman pulls the curtains and asks more questions.

They run tests for hours, or days, he isn't sure. Time lies around him like empty fields. He can walk the painted line. He can touch his nose and her nose back and forth. He identifies every animal and object on the cards and writes his name clearly.

You've filled an entire page with your signature! the doctor says, leaning over to see.

I love you, he says and takes hold of her breast.

Someone pulls his hand away.

For a while he's in a big room where he loves everybody. He tries to get close to them in the pressing together that brings such joy, only someone always moves him away.

One day David manages to walk out of the hospital. He steps into the road as if to greet the traffic and when a driver stops and tries to persuade him back onto the pavement, he punches her. Then he lies down. Several people drive round him, some taking pictures, before the hospital staff arrive.

The decision is made to move him to a secure residential unit across the city. Iris is asked to be present when he's put into the ambulance. She has a calming effect and there are many papers to sign. He has to be strapped into his seat – *like a cross between a baby and a lunatic* she says with a laugh to his sister, who stores this away as further evidence of Iris's cold heart.

Kate keeps asking Iris why they can't see him. She speaks quietly in long streams as if trying to wear away her mother's resistance but afraid of raising her voice.

He's better now. You said. He doesn't even have to stay in bed. We saw him when he had it, he practically died there right in front of us, remember? So why shouldn't we see him now?

He's very unhappy at the moment because he doesn't understand.

Understand what?

How to be.

Lou says much less. She hates how all this has made her mother look so small and sound so hollow.

What do you mean, *how to be*? What sort of fucking nonsense is that?

Iris reaches out her arms to Lou, who steps back.

He was supposed to have MS! What's a stroke got to do with it?

I don't know. I don't think anyone does. It may be connected, perhaps not.

What about the doctors? They're supposed to know! Did you know? That he was going to have a stroke? You know the symptoms, don't you? They're online!

Please don't go looking stuff up. You'll only scare yourselves.

We know what he'll be like. It says. You have to let us see him because we know. It fucking says.

Kate lines up beside her sister, looking just as coldly at Iris, whispering *It fucking says*.

Lou is shaking. Iris had been turning away just as she turned away from their questions when their father moved out, only this time Lou has stopped her. She has said what she wanted to say and for once her mother has listened. She has the words now, and the voice. What might she say next? They are all shaking.

Iris explains to the doctors that she and David had been in the process of a divorce and that his sister is responsible for all decisions regarding his care. She gives them her number. His sister turns up at the house one evening and they have a hissed conversation on the doorstep about why Iris won't let the girls see him.

They must lie awake at night imagining the worst, his sister says.

It is the worst.

Iris cannot bring herself to explain that David had decided not to come back, let alone why he had to leave, and so she must endure his family's judgement. If this had happened at his sister's, where after all he lived, she would have been the one who went to the hospital, signed the forms and answered the questions. Iris forwards letters from the hospital unopened.

The day after David had his stroke she kept picking up her phone and putting it down again, having forgotten who it was she meant to call. If she'd looked later, she would have seen that she rang Raif three times but she will have no memory of this. Her mind swept it aside even as she pressed the numbers. Otherwise she'd have to think about what it might mean.

She can't think about anything because life has become a hellish oscillation. David is and isn't dead. He is and isn't her husband. She loves him and she doesn't. She cannot after all recover her old life, nor can she anticipate a different one. For now Iris will be one of the people who go out into the city armoured against it. If she lets herself feel anything then she will have to feel something about this.

When Iris arrives at the secure unit, she's buzzed through one heavy glass door after another. She tells herself that it's not so bad. There are places to sit, even a small garden.

He won't wash, the nurse says. He's difficult to manage because he's still got his strength.

He seems very medicated.

We don't want to use restraints.

David has no grace now that he has no style. He looks peculiar and small. When he sees Iris he tries to leap up to prove the miracle of his recovery but there's a problem with distance. It takes so much longer for his hand to make contact or for his foot to reach the floor. And he's still in the waiting room. Isn't it time to go home? But the lovely woman is here. He wants to push himself inside her at any point he can find.

To Iris he looks both childish and geriatric as he rocks back and forth vaguely rubbing himself.

You need a shower, she says. I'll run it for you. Get undressed.

David doesn't want to undress because he's no longer

certain of his edges but now the woman is taking off his clothes and it's alright. His edges remain. Even so he refuses to be led towards the shower. *Fuck it*, she says, and starts to unbutton her top. Very quickly her body is there in front of him and he follows it. When she's under the falling water, he can't see her body any more and so he goes to find it.

Iris is shocked to find herself so close to him again. But it's not him. His breath has a metallic tang that is so alien to her that it makes her want to vomit. She craves the dry dark scent of his skin but when she presses her face to his chest, she smells onions, shellfish and milk. She knows this body better than any other. It hasn't outwardly changed. But her mind insists it's not him because it doesn't smell like him.

She takes a long time, making sure the water doesn't get in his eyes, flinching from nothing. His hands move towards her breasts but are too tired to reach them. He shoves his penis between her legs a few times but so vaguely that she barely registers it. She washes him until he smells of nothing and then she clings to him and weeps. The way David takes her head and presses it to his is so familiar that she wants to stay there forever, being held by him until they're both washed away.

She hardly sleeps and tries to exhaust herself by walking to work through the bare park under black trees, along grey streets. She pays a student to be there after school for the girls when David used to be and continues to move her debts from one card to another. The girls grow taller overnight.

Iris can admit that coming home is easier now that

David will never be there. She thinks of him as removed from their world – not in the end by her – and of herself as the engine of life for her girls.

Perhaps you should let them see him, says Max.

See what?

He's still himself, isn't he?

He's—

She's about to say that David is his animal self but that's not strictly true. He's a pathetically recognisable version of his human self. The girls would find it tormenting.

Iris focuses on her work. She spends a lot of time thinking about humidity and the abrasive qualities of dust but she also takes a speck of paint from a wooden mask, sets it in resin and has it scanned in an electron micro-scope. She then breaks down its components, cross-refer-ences and locates the mask to the east of Nigeria pre-1900. Today she is assessing items taken from a psychiatric ward in the 1940s which include thirty-six coat hangers, four skipping ropes and one game of snakes and ladders. She prefers paint and metal to organic materials that need so much protection from change. Anything once living cannot be fixed. Nothing will stop it breaking down.

the mortsafe

We open up the body in the hope of finding the truth or the future. Someone has to be willing to take another person apart, or at least able to stop thinking of them as a person. How do you accomplish this other than by repetition? You cut open bodies until you don't think of them as that. Henry VIII allowed the anatomy schools the bodies of four hanged criminals a year. Charles II increased this to six.

These dissections were carried out in public as if part of the punishment, *a further terror and peculiar mark of infamy*. Even if your body remained intact, in law it belonged to no one and so the bodysnatchers supplying anatomists in the nineteenth century were committing no crime. Like a psychoanalyst entering the mind, they tunnelled into the grave from imperceptible angles and drew out what they could, leaving no trace on the surface. There was plenty of demand for their services. The price of a corpse increased tenfold in twenty years.

A mortsafe was an iron grille or cage in which a coffin was placed before burial to protect the corpse from being taken. After six weeks or so, when the body had decayed beyond the point of being of any use to the anatomist, the mortsafe would be removed and hired out to someone else. The practice was for there to be two locks and for separate people to hold the keys.

The structures we borrow in order to protect ourselves cannot keep us intact. Our need for them reveals how vulnerable – or should that be susceptible – we are to being carried off, opened up, exposed.

the new

Perhaps falling in love in middle age is in part the desire to experience fixity again, to take hold of another so as to put ourselves in place. To do this we change how we live, what we enjoy, how we dress, who we spend time with, and we call this new.

In love we look mostly at ourselves and also at our lover. (Those who look only at their lover are using that love to turn away from themselves.) Our senses are turned up but at the same time we have difficulty absorbing those things that don't pertain. We feel strongly present in the world just as it ebbs away. Nothing can reach past this love. If danger comes, we have acquired immunity. The horror and despair that used to reach us as if they were our own are now distant scenes. Love makes us heartless.

Iris is being necessarily heartless. She can't stand what's happened to David or the idea that she somehow caused it. She's frightened by how much she felt when he pressed his head to hers in the shower. It was habit or reflex – not love. How could he now be capable of love? He has feelings and desires but no memory. Nothing builds. And what is love without a story? He cannot even name her.

His family describe him now as *harmless*, especially when encouraging Iris to take the girls to visit. There are ways in which he'll never hurt her again but he is not harmless. His helplessness is a form of tremendous power and she must cut herself off from this. She learnt to seal herself against each disappointment in their marriage. Faced with his new brutal presence in her life, she knows that she must feel nothing.

She falls through her thoughts at night and it is Raif who catches her. He helped her up when she fell down the station steps. His fingertip against her cheek steadied her. It's how she remembers them walking through the doorway at the museum – as a steadying.

One morning at breakfast, Kate asks a question.

Now that Dad has had a stroke, is he a rapist?

Of course not. What made you think that?

There was this man who had a stroke and he couldn't stop raping everyone.

Where?

Online.

What have you been looking at?

Not for the first time, Iris thinks she shouldn't let them have a computer in their room. Or that she should check the history and update the filters. But everyone says all that is pointless and the more you restrict them, the more they want to see. She doesn't want to think about what they might see.

Mum, says Lou. There was a woman who took her clothes off in public and when she wanted to pee she just did. Right where she was.

Didn't Dad do that? asks Kate.

We're not supposed to know about that! says Lou.

Yes, he did, says Iris.

Talking about this is better than talking about rape so she explains.

His brain injury means that he's forgotten how to behave. It's not his fault. He doesn't mean it. And yes, he did pee in front of everyone and that's how they knew what had happened to his brain. But who told you? I didn't.

We heard you on the phone.

We always hear you.

Well, you shouldn't listen.

We don't want to. We can't help it.

Kate starts to giggle. Lou too.

Did he really? Pee in front of the doctor and everyone?

Apparently. He walked over to the sink, peed and sat down again and carried on the conversation.

In front of people?

Yes.

Iris is laughing too. For the first time she isn't pretending anything to her children. They're just having a conversation.

a lapse

Winter gives way. Gales hurtle across the city. The wind swerves between buildings in concentrated gusts, reminding people that they live on a small island and that this city is right on the edge of it. A crane is blown over, scaffolding rattles, hoardings ripple and flap. But the sun that follows draws forth a pale edge of green, yellow and white which steadily brightens. Hearts quicken. The skies are moving again.

Raif visits his mother once a month, on a Saturday, arriving for lunch. Usually he stays the night. While Helen, alone in the flat in London, imagines him tucked up in a bed that's too small for him, surrounded by posters and toys, he's often out till the early hours. He'll text her the next day, on his way home, explaining that there's no signal at his mother's house and he's sorry not to have been in touch.

When he goes home, Raif encounters his sixteen-year-old self just as Helen envisages but not in the posters on his bedroom wall. As a teenager he found his town exciting and regularly frightening. All the underground activity that melts into city life is difficult to hide in a small place on the sea edge. He was tolerated by a gang of boys who wandered the streets seeking out dark corners. They observed deals being struck for sex or drugs. They loitered opposite a house where the front door hung off its hinges and sheets were pinned across the windows. They knew whose number was given in the small ad in the local paper offering home massage – or they said they did, nudging each other and pointing at the town's one traffic warden as she passed by. They followed exhausted women and wary men and heard them speak in tongues. These strangers had arrived in their town as if risen from the sea and they believed that to live by the sea was to see a richer side of life.

Raif tells his mother he's off to the pub to catch up with some old friends. Out of tact, Bridget doesn't ask who. There weren't any particular friends she can recall. The landlord and the regulars remember him and nod hello but no one starts a conversation.

One night he looks up from his drink and there she is: Leigh, the queen of the girls, the one who offered herself as a girlfriend after his father died. He was stupid about it and didn't understand. It's her – the same emphatic stance and square shoulders, the tightly cut denim jacket, the high ponytail of black hair and she's turning towards him and oh god the same rosy face and wide mouth but, he actually shakes himself, of course it isn't her. That was some twenty-five years ago and this girl's twenty at most. Someone says something and the girl laughs and her hand flies up to cover her mouth. The same laugh, the same gesture – Raif's body is exploding with the force of recognition. She's walking towards him now, no, past him, and their eyes meet and there's . . . nothing. Her body is telling her nothing at all. Why should it? She doesn't know him.

Raif stays where he is, almost daring to imagine that she might come back. He drinks fake brands of vodka and lager, and plays pool with himself on the warped table. At midnight he's sitting on a concrete bench on the sea wall. He has a half-bottle of whisky in his pocket but hasn't drunk much of it. He never does. It's more of a prop, something he would have offered the gang while they stood around in the cold. He's at the opposite end of town to his home, which is at the golf course, library end. This is the car park, caravan, nightclub, games hall end and much of it is derelict. Even the sea seems to have forgotten what it's for and slops uncertainly against the shingle.

Is he still waiting for the girl to come back? It's colder than he'll admit and there's nothing to watch, no one about. Eventually he sets off home and, turning a corner, he sees her again – the denim jacket, the high ponytail. Without thinking, he runs to catch her up. She turns, ready to shout, and then she laughs, her hand to her mouth, and shakes her head.

I know you, don't I?

It's not the girl in the pub but it is Leigh. Her face isn't rosy, her mouth is thin and her hair a flat chemical black scraped back from white roots.

It's me, from school, remember? You gave me such a shock!

Of course, he says and she kisses him on the cheek just as he tries to shake her hand.

You haven't changed much, she says. I mean, your hair's gone a bit and you've put on a bit but no, you haven't changed.

This really is Leigh, which means that he, like her, is past forty and not fourteen. He ends up walking her home, where, she explains, she lives with her daughter. People think they're sisters. She invites him in, makes coffee and he pulls the whisky from his pocket, which is just the kind of lordly gesture he dreamt of making back then.

Here he is, alone, late at night, with the queen of the girls! She asks him methodically about his life and when he gets to the part about his wife having died, she starts to cry. He's used to this and waits for her to reach out a hand and say something consoling.

Only she doesn't. Leigh isn't crying for the beautiful boy who didn't know who he was but because he has brought back a time when life coursed through her. When he spoke of his dead wife she could think only of her own deadness. She's forgotten that he's there.

Raif wonders if he ought to find out why she's so sad but the idea tires him. He holds her hand for a while and then gets up and says that it's been lovely to see her and he leaves. Later he realises that she never said his name. He's right – she didn't remember it.

Leigh's sadness makes him want to reassure himself that his life is brightly lit and peopled. In the morning he calls Helen as soon as he wakes and asks her to come down for lunch. His mother, he says, is dying to meet her.

Helen decides not to wonder why she's being invited down so suddenly (or why there is now enough phone signal for Raif to call). She brings flowers.

Look, Mum, says Raif. Tulips from Helen.

Bridget is sitting on a bench in the garden. She has

closed her eyes and is enjoying the sun on this prematurely springlike day. Her garden is already erupting with crocuses and narcissi. She doesn't need flowers. She passes the tulips to Raif without looking.

Put them in something, she says.

Helen notices that Bridget pronounces his name differently – *Ryeef* – but she won't remark on it. Meeting his mother is a big step and she doesn't want to ruin it. (When did she become so tentative?)

You have a lovely garden, she says.

Bridget nods. This is a nice thing for the girl to say, only she doesn't stop there. She goes on.

Really lovely. So cared for, so cleverly laid out.

Snake's head fritillaries, Bridget says to shut her up.

Really? Do please show me.

Not yet, of course. In May. You'll have to come back then to see them. Will you?

I'd love to!

I don't think so.

Raif looks at his watch.

Mum, do you want me to do anything about lunch?

Lunch? Bridget wonders.

He means baste the roast or put in the potatoes. He hasn't noticed that nothing has happened in the kitchen today. He made himself toast and coffee, went for a walk and met Helen at the station, having left his mother a note: *I've invited a friend called Helen down for lunch. Please don't go to any trouble.*

You didn't see the note, did you? says Raif. I'm so sorry. Why don't I take you both out? What do you feel like,

Mum? A roast at The Berkshire Arms or fish at Sarsons?

Bridget opens her eyes.

Snake's head fritillaries.

Helen can tell that something's not right. It's as if Bridget keeps meeting dead ends in herself. Why hadn't Raif warned her? Because Raif has seen nothing. His mother is his mother. He sees what he remembers seeing and hasn't noticed the clutter becoming chaos and the time it takes her to complete the journey from one room to the next.

Bridget stands up, crosses the lawn and prods at something in a bed.

Helen starts to say something.

I didn't know, she begins.

Know what, says Raif.

It's not a question. She decides to change the subject and so says what she meant not to.

That your name is really pronounced *Ryeef*.

It's not.

But your mother—

She didn't say it like that. She said it properly.

In the kitchen Helen sees the note Raif left for Bridget that morning. *A friend called Helen.* What had he said? *My mother is dying to meet you.* Bridget has no idea who she is.

On the train home Raif sits opposite and studies Helen while she reads a magazine. His mother seems not to like her. The triplets responded in the same way. And what does he know? He mistook a teenager for her mother. He did not know his wife. He has become so uncertain that he cannot form a view of his own. He looks at Helen and wonders if he knows her. What has he missed?

He's looking for an explanation for a lapse in – what? Confidence? Judgement? Feeling? All he knows is that he's not sure and can't act. So he listens more carefully than he should to what others say and his own idea of Helen stalls just as it should be building.

I can't say

Iris is at home, on the phone to an old friend who lives on the other side of the world. She has to tell him what's happened to David and does so as lightly as she can.

At least he doesn't feel sorry for himself any more, she laughs.

Lou is sitting at the kitchen table doing her homework. As soon as Iris is off the phone, she starts to yell.

Don't do that! Don't talk about my father like that!

I didn't mean—

Like he's a joke! You always have. Even when he had MS you were horrible. Making him do stuff and shouting all the time.

That's not—

Maybe he had the stroke because you were so cross!

You don't understand.

That's the point! I do. And so does Kate.

There's stuff you don't know.

Like what?

I can't say.

That's just an excuse.

I love your father but he—

He got ill.

But he also—

No! I don't want to know about your private stuff! He got ill and nothing else is as bad as that and if you'd been nice . . .

It's exactly what David would have said. *Why can't you be nice?* Lou goes off to her room before Iris can respond.

An hour later Lou comes to find her mother but hangs back in the doorway. There's such weather passing through her stiff little face that Iris wants to take her in her arms but she hesitates. She feels respectful of her daughter and no longer sure how to approach her. Iris of the layers and walls sees that Lou is starting to form her own.

What Lou wants to say is that she's sorry for shouting at her mother. Also that while she's sad about her father, she's glad that neither of her parents is pretending any more that they're alright. And anyway she and Kate have done a lot of pretending too. About stuff they've heard and seen.

She wants to explain that being at home is like being dead and all her life is out there at school, with her friends and this boy she passes on the stairs on a Tuesday afternoon between science and maths. He was at her bus stop the other day when she knows he goes home in the opposite direction.

She wants to speak of her body and how she can't look in a mirror because she doesn't recognise herself and nothing looks like it does online. Adolescence is moving towards her and part of her is rushing to greet it while another insists that this is too soon. She wants above all to stop herself telling her mother that she's found a photo.

Lou and Kate are too old for hide-and-seek but they've made the game into a family joke. Lou always hides under David's desk because she intends to be found as quickly as possible. Kate knows this and refuses to find her so Lou gets to spend some quiet time curled up under the desk. After shouting at Iris, that was where Lou had gone.

Everything in that floor-level landscape was familiar to her: the wonky desk leg and the broken box file, the holes in the carpet and the folded piece of card. Now that her mind is rushing about naming and probing, her hand reached out and picked the card up.

It was a photo of a woman. She wasn't particularly young or old or pretty, and she was sitting on a beach. In a big coat, not a bikini, but all the same Lou could tell that the photo was private. It'd been folded up and then hidden. Not hidden. It had slipped down here and not been looked for. Or not found. This was her father's desk and she knew from the atmosphere she grew up in, the tight voices of her parents and the words they used, that no one wanted to find this woman. She didn't need to be in a bikini because the look on her face made it clear. She was smiling as if she'd won something.

Kate and Lou believe that information is its own solution but now Lou knows something she doesn't want to. What should she do with the photo? She can't put it back because Iris works at this desk now. And it doesn't feel safe to throw it in a bin, not even a bin in the street in case someone finds it who knows her mother – or who is her mother. So she carries it up to Kate and says that she has an object for the museum. Kate opens the cupboard. In addition to the lead to David's phone charger there's a disposable razor, a travelcard and a button from one of his sludge-lemon shirts. Each has a date and number written on a slip beside it. Lou unfolds the photo and passes it to

Kate, who folds it up again and puts it in the cupboard, her ten-year-old mind rushing past what it might mean.

So Iris is right that Lou has a secret and doesn't want to share it. She tells Lou that she's sorry and Lou says she knows.

the object reminds us

Iris is leaving work when the seed of a migraine starts to burrow behind her left eye. She takes the pink pills. Within the hour, just as she reaches home, a blanket will be laid across her brain and she'll be able to sleep. She's on the street when she remembers that the debate she promised to take part in at Raif's college is tonight. She had an email only a week ago from the person organising it, which she'd skimmed over because she was too tired to think about it. But it's not like her to forget anything so completely, especially not the debate which had been their excuse if not for meeting then for meeting again.

Why did she agree to take part? She finds it hard enough to speak in public without having someone argue against her. She has to call the student looking after the girls and hope she can stay on and then get across the city in thirty minutes, which is just possible. Tonight there's a train waiting on the platform when she arrives. She settles down to make some notes but halfway through the journey it occurs to her that she's travelling towards Raif, who she hasn't seen since . . . when?

She lets herself remember now that she rang him – god knows why – when David had his stroke, but left no message. She tried three times before she calmed down and remembered that she didn't have any real claim on his attention. They were colleagues who'd enjoyed a flirtation, nothing more. He hadn't returned her calls and soon the tension and excitement his presence brought her evaporated. If she thought of him at all it was as the person she was doing this favour for – taking part in the debate. Now it seems she's even forgotten that.

The city is moving her towards him too easily, too quickly, and Iris is finding it difficult to breathe. She gets off at the next stop and walks the rest of the way so that by the time she arrives, the debate has begun. She's hurried in and seated between two academics she doesn't know. The first speaker from the opposite panel is mid-argument. It's Meike, the majestic student who can't see. There's a large audience and the people either side of her look well prepared. She can't stop herself scanning the room. Where is Raif? Meike is coming to her conclusion.

The objects we put in museums are representative, evocative, metaphorical . . . therefore they are about the idea of themselves. We don't need to preserve their actual matter, which is inherently unstable. We shouldn't be putting our dwindling resources into trying to keep materials stable when we can capture and store images of every aspect of them, on any scale.

Iris is being introduced. She has to speak but the pills she took are beginning to blur her thoughts. When she was walking along the river talking to Raif, it had been easy. They argued as a form of flirtation. But what is she to say here? And where is he?

She has the notes she began on the train but sets them aside. She wants to argue with Meike.

I would suggest that precisely because we can capture images of every aspect of an object, we need to preserve the object itself.

The audience are waiting for her to explain.

The more people learn only from images, the less idea they will have of the object.

Meike looks baffled or startled, Iris can't tell but she's starting to hate her. She tries again.

The object reminds us—

The man on her left coughs. Is he trying not to laugh?

The object reminds us that it is after all an object. Not an image or a description but a thing.

This feels utterly true to Iris, but it sounds too simple to satisfy the room. They wait.

I think what you're trying to say— begins the man on her left.

He goes on to speak for fifteen minutes without pause. Iris isn't insulted, she's relieved. When it's over she makes herself go up to Meike, to say hello and to thank her (she ought to thank someone) but she says something else.

I thought Raif was taking part in this? I mean, what I mean is, he was the one who—

Meike takes her time.

Hello. I hope you enjoyed that. We did so appreciate your contribution. Raif? Didn't someone say? He had a family emergency.

Iris tries not to think about the tall, uncertain Helen.

What's happened?

Meike shrugs.

They wouldn't tell me, would they?

But who would they tell?

Iris wants Meike to meet her eyes so badly that she refuses to believe she can't. Only now does she catch herself.

I just mean it would have been good to know, beforehand, that he wasn't taking part. Someone should have said.

I'm sorry if you were inconvenienced but it was all very last-minute and we did so value your contribution.

Iris says something about getting home for the children and makes her way patiently back across the city. She needs time to compose herself and to get Raif back in place, in the past, in the life before David's stroke, which is not her life now.

alarms

Raif is not at the debate because Helen rings to say that his mother has turned up at the flat and seems agitated.

She calms down when he appears, says she's starving and then shakes her head at the plate put in front of her. Eventually she picks up a piece of chicken and gnaws on it briefly before wiping her hands on her blue silk shirt. She smiles at Helen like a guilty child but when Raif asks if she'd like coffee, her usual expression snaps back into place.

Lovely!

She doesn't drink it.

Raif takes Bridget through to the sofa bed and watches while she unpacks her little case. She has everything she needs, neatly folded, and he is reassured. Evidently she just got in a muddle about dates. He starts to clear up in the kitchen but Helen says she'll do it, he must need some rest. When he turns on the bedroom light Bridget is there in the bed, sitting up and smiling. The stained silk shirt looks dangerously loose.

Mum, this is my—

Did you see the moon?

In the moment it takes him to come up with a reply, he makes a massive adjustment. His mother is not herself and never will be again. He must take her hand now and lead her through whatever comes next. He will have to think about her, plan for her and decide for her. He cannot be uncertain now.

Come and show me the moon, he says. No, stay there. It's a cold night. I'll fetch your dressing gown.

When he reappears she gets up and he sees – but tries hard not to – that her lower half is naked. She steps calmly into the dressing gown.

Is it a cold night, darling?

Yes, Mum. It's a very cold night.

In the hallway Bridget stops.

What was it I wanted?

Raif takes her arm.

Weren't you about to brush your teeth?

When she's finished he leads her back to the sofa bed and says goodnight.

In the morning Bridget is up first, sitting at the empty kitchen table, still wearing the shirt with the chicken grease on the front.

Have you seen the moon? she says, going to the window. Come and look. Now where's it gone?

Doesn't the moon sleep in the day?

She shakes her head over and over and then starts to shout.

No no no no!

Raif takes his frightened little mother in his arms and tells her that it's alright, it doesn't matter, it's all going to be alright.

He rearranges his classes and takes her home, having made an emergency appointment with her doctor. If he can reassure her about each small step, she seems content.

What are you looking at? The moon. Where are we going? Home.

He talks to social services and care agencies, and they make a plan to install alarms. Someone will come in each day to make sure she's eating and hasn't had a fall. He's shocked by agency fees. Will they have to sell the house? Her carer calls to say she won't eat her lunch or a neighbour to report that she's been peeing in the garden. He's learning that this happens everywhere. Memory gives way and a person stops being able to moderate themselves according to the world.

There is the ice over the deep lake of loving and losing his wife, and there is the bed of that lake which is the death of his father. Where is his mother? Is she withdrawing or being withdrawn? She has always been there to move away from, encouraging him to make his own life. Now she has started to move away from him. He can already see her growing smaller, edging out onto the ice.

The triplets live twenty miles away and one of them brings their mother, Sorcha, to visit Bridget each week.

We're family, says Ashley when she has to report that they found a pan boiled dry on the stove. We can manage. When's the alarm system being put in?

I don't want to worry you, says Jessica, but Bridget was out in the street in the night shouting about a fire. She locked herself out. You can't rely on neighbours to sort out things like that.

Raif cancels another class and gets on another train. He finds his mother in the garden. She is barefoot, and her hands and face are smeared with earth.

There you are, she says, reaching out her mucky fingers.

Her brain moves to protect her from the knowledge that it's dying and so she makes sense of his appearing by deciding she has summoned him.

You're late. Aren't you late?

I was worried. You didn't answer your phone.

I had to divide these irises.

She's standing on some geraniums and around her lies the wreckage of her irises. Every root ball has been dug up and split but nothing has been replanted.

Where did you find the strength to do all this? You must be exhausted.

What do you mean?

Raif goes to make tea and finds her mobile, switched off, in a kitchen cupboard. So she knows how to switch it off. She doesn't want to use it. Why not just say? At some level she's doing these things on purpose.

He stays for two hours, because that seems a reasonable length of time, but the visit is not a success. He tries to talk about the things they've always talked about. Not just family and the weather but her work and his. He tells her about the museum stores, where his friend works, and how they have all these old X-ray machines.

Some of them are almost a hundred years old, so you were probably using them when you started out!

I wasn't working a hundred years ago.

I know. That was a joke.

I hadn't qualified then so I couldn't have used those machines.

Would you like to see them? I brought you some pictures.

Raif opens his laptop but Bridget has spotted something stuck to the sofa and becomes absorbed in trying to scrape it off.

Don't you want to see the pictures?

No, I don't.

But I want to show them to you.

He'd spent an afternoon preparing this, pleased to think he was being a good son and anticipating her pleasure. Bridget is still picking at the sofa.

This might come off with a little vinegar.

I could take you on a special visit. Because of my friend, who works for the museum. You could see all the old machines.

There are better machines now.

I just thought. The history might—

You were always good at history.

It's what I teach.

Do you? That's nice.

But what I'm suggesting is—

Are you going now?

Going?

Yes.

Unless you want me to stay?

Not really.

The unsettlement of Bridget's mind leads to collapsed bridges and fallen walls but also to clearings. Like a child she believes in how she feels. She can say that she is tired, hungry or cold. That she wants someone to stay or go. But there are the forces that drive her into the night or that creep up behind her and these she cannot express.

Nor can her son bring himself to say what he needs. So he stages his own emergency by ignoring a chest infection until it becomes pneumonia. Now he's too sick to visit his mother.

The days that follow are happy ones. Helen cares for him but sleeps elsewhere so he can lie in the lake of himself, so worn out by each aching breath that he can put nothing into words. Usually his mind rushes ahead of his words, evaluating impact and pitfalls. Now he doesn't have the energy. They just talk. He's practical about his mother and seems to have cast off his grief. Helen relaxes. Raif finds himself wanting to reach her.

the iron lung

Does Raif want Helen to do his breathing for him? There are times when we need someone to run us for a while so that we can take a rest. People fall in love just to bring this about. They find someone they know will take over.

One of the ugliest objects in the museum, and one Iris is particularly fond of, is the iron lung. Built in the 1930s, it's seven feet long and weighs around eight hundred pounds. It looks like an early space rocket or submarine and, like them, provides a place in which to breathe. The patient is sealed inside the iron lung up to their neck. A pump sucks out the air, lowering the pressure and forcing their lungs to expand. Then the air is pumped back in, forcing their lungs to compress.

It's a brute operation: the pump clunks and the air is drawn through what sounds like the narrowest of apertures. The machine sounds desperate: as if, like the patient's body, it's being forced to keep going. It makes a noise that travels through the teeth and skull of the listener. Whatever rate the machine is set at, its breath sounds unnatural – neither fast nor slow, only horribly inexorable. Forcing the body to keep breathing can damage it even more. The lungs look strong, like a pair of bellows, but they are made up of tiny fragilities.

There are people who have spent most of their lives in an iron lung. They contracted polio in the 1950s and have been unable to breathe unaided ever since. Imagine being locked into something that you can never fully enter. You are outside it from the neck up. Do you separate yourself or do you eventually incorporate it into your sense of who you are?

The iron lung was replaced by a practice of diverting the blood to a machine that removes carbon dioxide and adds oxygen. It has made a vital difference to the prognosis of victims of the new types of flu. Does this mean that the act of breathing could become superfluous? And if so, how do we now define the moment of death? Will we have no clear end?

questions

In the city it's not difficult to see the adjustments people have made. Some have locked up part of themselves as if in a separate room. Others multiply and set off in several directions at once. There are those who leave themselves behind or meet themselves in a place they swear they've never been.

Since David's stroke, his brain has concentrated on what it can still manage. His thoughts go where they can and conserve their resources. He doesn't like this doctor. She asks questions that he knows the answers to but tricks him into saying the wrong thing.

Are you familiar with the saying *a rolling stone gathers no moss?*

David nods.

What does it mean? she asks.

He doesn't look at her because she has the shape that pulls him. And he wants to get this right. He knows it.

Moss is slow. The stone is gone.

The doctor is about to speak but pauses and then starts again.

What might we be trying to express when we say it?

Moss is in the earth. Not the stone.

Which is true, but what are we trying to express, about ourselves, when we use this saying?

Moss can't move. A stone can.

The doctor makes a note and consults her list.

Good. Now could you complete this sentence: He posted a letter without a . . .

Stamp.

Very good. Now can you complete it again but use a word that doesn't make sense.

He posted a letter without a . . . stamp. Sorry. He posted a letter without a st— He posted a letter without a . . . without a . . . Sorry, so sorry, the word—

David knows what he's being asked to do. The sentence lays itself out in front of him like a short straight path but when he reaches the last word, something shoves him back to *stamp*.

Fuck it! Jesus! Fuck it! David is punching his head.

You're doing very well, David. This isn't a test. No right or wrong. One last question, can you tell me something that isn't true?

Three times David starts to speak and stops again.

That the . . . my name is . . . ridiculous . . . Fuck it . . . Sorry . . . Ridiculous . . .

You must need some rest. Let's finish there.

But David is still punching his head, which doesn't feel like his at all.

what's missing, what remains

Easter comes in March and Iris, who can only take half the holiday off work, sends Kate and Lou to a drama club which finishes at three. They can walk home and make themselves tea and toast. She can be back by six. They're so capable and there are two of them so she has no qualms. On the second day, she receives a call from the drama club. Are they not well? The auditions are that afternoon and they'd seemed so keen. She tells the tutor that she's on her way but is not sure where she should go. She starts to ring David and then remembers. Who should she ring? The police? No. The girls are probably at home. Perhaps one of them is, as the tutor said, unwell.

She forgets whatever she's supposed to be doing that afternoon – two meetings and a conservation estimate on a key exhibit – and runs out of the building and into the street, where she finds a taxi and tells the driver it's an emergency, her children are . . . are what? They're not at home but they've left her a note. It says they've gone to see their father and will be back by five o'clock. They are using their own money and have researched the route online.

Iris was told within weeks of David's stroke that he was unlikely ever to leave secure care. But it has taken some time for her to be able to keep this in view. Kate and Lou must remember their father as himself and not the border-less creature he has become. Besides which, he might not recognise them as his daughters and how might he behave then? They must never see their father again.

Iris phones the unit and they say that the girls have arrived and no, they will not be given access to their father without her permission, nor should they leave the building without her. She says she's on her way.

The girls are waiting in the visitors' room, where there is a television, comics and games. They were so distressed when no one would let them see their father that one of the doctors had come to talk to them.

I'm sorry, she said. But there are strict rules. We need your mother's permission.

Is that true of seeing everyone in hospital ever? asked Lou.

No. But some patients, those who have been acutely ill, who need a lot of rest or who are not themselves . . . It's for everyone's good.

He's our dad! shouted Kate.

No, said Lou. He's not. She said he's not himself.

Well, who is he, then? yelled Kate. You're yourself, aren't you, unless you're dead? Aren't you?

Lou did what her mother would have done and took her sister in her arms. The doctor's bleeper went off and she got up to leave. Lou stood up too.

If we were your kids and he was your husband, what would you do? Would you let us see him?

The doctor tried to give as much information as people asked for. These girls weren't children. They were smart and they were so distressed. She started to shrug.

Tell my mum, said Kate. Make her understand.

When Iris arrives, the girls are so righteous that she forgets to be cross with them.

They said we could see him.

If you said we could.

You just need to say we can.

We know what he'll be like, remember? We've seen it online.

They are ten and twelve years old and think that they know the world because they've seen it. They've looked at brain scans and read about miracles. They've watched a man drilling into his own head and a woman talk about how she tried to chop off her arm because it didn't belong to her.

Iris speaks to the doctor and agrees that they can see David. They're taken through a series of doors to another room where armchairs and side tables are lined up along two walls. A nurse goes to collect David and there he is, their father, only he's quite different. He's not like any of the people they saw online. His face isn't lopsided and he doesn't limp. But he's wearing funny clothes and looks really tired and he needs a haircut. Lou and Kate watch as the nurse leads him to a chair. The nurse goes to the door but doesn't leave. Iris hopes the girls won't ask why.

No one moves. Iris thought the girls would rush to him but they stay in their chairs. They pull out their phones and don't look up again.

Iris stops herself telling them to say hello, to give him a kiss, but she tries to encourage them by going to kiss David herself. His hand moves towards her breast as she steps away.

Hello, David. I brought Kate and Lou to see you.

Kate and Lou, he says.

The sedation means that each word takes its time but his voice is still his voice.

Hello, Daddy, mutters Kate, still not looking up. Lou follows in quick echo.

Kate and Lou, he says again.

And then only raw noise as a spasm goes through his body.

Iris looks to the nurse, who has taken a step forward but makes a reassuring gesture with his hand.

Don't worry, Iris says to the girls. Sometimes we have feelings we can't express, especially if we're having trouble with words.

It is David who responds.

Trouble with words. We worry. Kate and Lou.

I think what your father means is—

Can we go now? asks Lou.

Kate is already on her feet.

Can we go back to that other room and get a drink?

Hello, Daddy! He barks it and, sliding down his chair, splays his legs and scratches his balls.

The girls freeze. Iris has to push them out of the room.

David is never going to be alright and he is never coming home and Iris needs to make this real. She opens his filing cabinet and hauls its contents onto the floor. She's not going to look at anything, just box it up quickly and put it away. But there are cards and notes tucked among bank statements, photographs too. They're at least ten years old. Not because David stopped what he did but because all that flirting and murmuring went online.

Lou comes into the room and stands between Iris and the heap of paper.

Why are you throwing everything away?

We need space.

What for?

I don't know. In case Granny comes to stay?

She never does. No one does. Why don't they?

Lou is frightening herself as well as Iris. Why can't she stop herself saying these things? Words bubble up and escape her and they hurt her mother and that is awful but also why she says them. She needs to hurt her mother.

I'm using this desk now, says Iris. It was mine, you know, originally. I need it for when I work at home.

But you work in the museum or the stores.

If you were sick or off school, I'd have to work at home. That's what single parents do.

You're not single.

Iris is kneeling on the floor in front of this terrible truth-telling daughter.

And you shouldn't go through his things, says Lou as she walks out. They're private.

Two weeks later Iris takes the girls to see him again. They sit there playing games on their phones. David looks only at Iris, who talks and talks. She tells him about the objects she's working on, how the weather has been so strange and who has been appointed to run the gallery he hates so much. Expressions pass across his face half-formed. He might be about to smile or cry or speak but he doesn't.

After ten minutes the girls ask if they can go and get a drink. They take Iris's money without looking at David. She knows they won't come back and that they'll want her to bring them again in a few weeks' time.

She asks the nurse to leave her and David alone for a minute, which he does. There are so many things to say.

I said you could come back, David. Even after everything. And you said – you said – and we agreed. We were ended. We'd decided and agreed but we didn't say. So no one knows and they think I'm just—

Pain is spiralling out of her and where is David to stop it? He was the one who stopped it. But he cannot divert, console or fuck her now. She starts to repeat herself, shouting because he seems so far away. In the end she's just making noise.

David keeps staring at her, drowsily astonished that the lovely woman is here again, although she's being quite tiring. What is this question? What is the answer? He doesn't know what she wants him to say. In the end he shrugs.

Iris sees a familiar gesture: the shrug that evaporated the panic she'd felt on the train stuck in the tunnel, that lightened her mood and made things possible, that meant it was alright not to say yes or no as there were other more interesting responses. But it was also the shrug that deflected her first enquiry – *Have you slept with someone else?* – and that met her questions about what they were

231

going to do about childcare or the leaking roof or the fact that he didn't have a proper job. It was an affectation and it was all that was left of him. The most real thing about him – a shrug.

She's wrong. David really doesn't know and is trying his best to say so.

the jealousy glass

We see with two eyes and receive two images but compound them into one. We need to be as definite as we can about where we are and what's around us. But what if we can see in more than one way at once? Does this enlarge the picture or confuse it?

Iris and Raif are living in a time of glances, when eyes flit and etiquette is lax. It's easy, perhaps too easy, for us to look wherever we want. We don't look for too long at another person unless we're trying to communicate interest or hostility, either to a heightened degree. Three hundred years ago the atmosphere in a room would have been more formal, more fraught. Public space was an opportunity for concealed communication. (Go out into the city and you will see that it still is.) Consider all that can happen in a crowded room.

The jealousy glass looks like nothing much: a small telescope used to see the action onstage more closely. The one in the museum, early eighteenth century, is fashioned from dark ivory and has a sharkskin case. It looks designed for discretion, being dull and unadorned. The image enters through a hole in the side and is deflected by a mirror onto the lens: *by which she could take a View of any Person she pleased without his having the least Suspicion of it, as the Glass was directed quite another Way.*

We are aware when crossing the city that our image is

being fixed continually by cameras – those we see and those we don't. To a large extent we must set this aside just as we cannot always wonder what someone might have glimpsed in us. But we still don't expect to be observed by someone who has turned away. Or to be able to pursue someone while averting our gaze. How much more potent they become. Perhaps it's safer not to be able to see them at all.

whose story?

Raif is determining his life with Helen. He wants it to be calm and complete. He has come to the end of Liis's death at last and realises he's glad that Helen is still here. He can see how withheld he has been because now he isn't. He's reaching out of himself, wanting contact so that he can go on building feeling. He swims each morning in the dilapidated college pool and carries its rhythm into his day so that life feels relaxed and generous. He's happy in a way he can't remember having been and easily satisfied. Things taste, feel and sound good.

Since last summer I have been coming back to life, he thinks, and then wonders if he's ever felt as alive before. He gathers up this happiness and tries to apply it to Helen.

She's touring with a drama group that visits prisons and he makes a point of turning up at both the showcase and the farewell party. The other actors tell Helen how proud Raif looks and it's true that he stands beside her, for the first time, as if he feels lucky to be there. He takes her to buy a new bed and doesn't correct the salesman who calls her *your wife*. He asks after her friends and remembers her stories. And he likes her to go with him to see Bridget, who now treats him like a stranger. He cries in front of Helen about how this makes him feel and she's able to console him.

One day he receives a message.

Hello, shadow man. I arrive on Friday. I will be wearing my silver coat and I have a story to tell. You promised me cherry blossom, remember?

It takes Raif a moment to realise that this is from the woman in the silver coat. He hasn't thought about her for months.

Ava is older than him – five or fifteen years, he can't tell. She's a professor of economics, recently widowed or is it divorced? He remembers a fine figure in a plum-coloured dress, chestnut hair put up in a complicated knot and a strong sexual gravity. When they met in that bar, they flirted intensively for a couple of hours and then Raif felt so sad and drunk that he'd started to cry. He told her about Liis and her father's defection, and how he didn't know if it really was her story.

Do you need to know? Ava asked.

I think so.

Then why not try to find out?

The decision he'd made not to confront Liis, not to break the surface on which they built their life, had hardened into a belief. It was not possible.

When the bar closed, he offered to walk Ava home but she said that as he had no idea where he was, she would walk him back to his hotel instead. She buttoned her silver coat and slipped her arm through his. At the hotel she kissed his cheek, accepted his card and turned to go. He could not let her.

Ava! he called after her.

She stopped and turned. He had no idea what to say.

I like your coat!

236

She laughed, shook her head and walked away.

At a safe distance they'd written every day then twice a week then a dashed line here and there before Raif, absorbed in his mother's needs and his ambitions for a life with Helen, didn't notice that their correspondence had petered out. Now here she is, in his city, expecting to meet. He offers dinner, even though it might suggest more than he intends, because to encounter her in daylight would be too much. They'd met in a dim bar and walked through streets that were more or less unlit. His fantasies, in which she joins him in the hotel, have been just as softly lit.

Now he's sitting opposite her in a restaurant and he's not sure why. He orders a salad and a small glass of wine and Ava, after conveying her disappointment, follows suit. They talk about their institutions and the funding of the humanities until Ava reminds him that she has a story to tell. She emanates the same delicious combination of calm and erotic force that he remembers but he feels exposed. Why did he tell her his most private thoughts? We walk away from such conversations presuming that our secrets will remain where we left them – in a dark bar we'll never return to. We don't think of the person we confided in carrying our secrets home, let alone bringing them back to us later. Ava doesn't hesitate to do exactly this.

I looked into what you told me. About your wife.

My wife?

Your wife. Her father's defection. It wasn't—

Something has started to move and he's not ready.

You did what?

You said you wanted to know but you couldn't bring yourself to do anything about it. I thought that as a friend—

A friend?

Raif wishes this woman had confined herself to his fantasies, naked under her silver coat in the dim hotel room.

I don't understand, Ava says. I made an enquiry. I was given some information. I thought it would help you.

He wants at least to be polite.

It would. I'm sorry if you feel—

The English apology.

I want to apologise for that too, but it would mean saying sorry again.

The English joke.

I'm not—

English? Yes you are. So English.

Their food arrives and they sit and look at it. Raif makes a decision.

I think I want to know. Please. I really do. I want to know.

Ava picks up her knife and fork and puts them down again.

Her father was a diplomat and when she was a teenager he was posted to New York and he got permission for one of his children to visit him.

So it's true.

It's not true that he defected. That is someone else's story.

But she stayed in America. That must be true.

It is. She ran away.

Raif's mind moves towards the facts, for they are facts now. Liis went to America and she ran away.

She must have been desperate, he says, and so brave.

I expect so.

Didn't her father try to find her?

Ava pauses. She's looking at him now.

He was sent home. He never recovered. He killed himself.

The ice breaks. Raif has been plunged into deep cold water by this person who . . . who is she?

Who are you to bring me this?

I thought I was a friend.

Raif speaks very quietly.

We barely know each other. That's why I told you my wife's story and my private doubts. Because you are nothing to do with my life. Only you seem to know more about my life than I do. Haven't you got a life of your own?

This is a voice he uses when someone crosses a line he's depending on. Like Helen at the party when he wasn't ready to admit who she was. *I'd like another glass of wine. Then get one.*

Ava flinches and then laughs. Another thought occurs to him.

Or did you think it would make an interesting piece of research?

She takes her time pouring a glass of water.

It is part of the story of my country. It also happens to be part of the story of your marriage.

I didn't know!

So I have given this to you.

I hadn't said I wanted you to go looking for it.

They drink in silence.

Do you remember, she says in her old warm voice, how you were when you came into that bar? You were full of your loss. It was your only subject. I felt sorry for you but you were quite boring.

You walked me back to my hotel.

You are a handsome man.

You sent messages every day.

Not for long.

She eats her salad. Raif stares at the dark window behind her. It occurs to him that now it would be better to know as much as he can. He remembers the conversation he had with Liis's sister.

Did the family blame her? he asks.

How would I know?

I think they did. How did she manage to stay in America?

Ava pushes her plate away. She looks hurried or bored, he can't tell.

Who knows, she says and picks up her bag. I'm sorry that the story has turned out to be so sad.

Did you not think you should have asked me before—

You said you wanted to know. And why do you think of it as your story? Which part of it is about you? She wasn't only your wife.

He pays the bill. She does not thank him as she leaves.

Raif isn't ready to think about what she has told him. He spends the rest of the evening in a pub he dislikes and then makes his way home as slowly as possible. He kisses Helen, goes into the bedroom, shuts the door and gets out the box of Liis's papers. Among them is an old address book. He knows what he's looking for as soon as he sees it – an American number under a name he never heard her mention, Erik. He wants to call it but what will he say?

Forgive this intrusion, he rehearses out loud . . . You don't know me but . . . I'm looking for Erik . . . My wife was a friend of Erik's. I have some news for him . . .

He calls the number but the line is dead.

the black place

Helen has lived with someone before. They split up when she was thirty and looking back she's amazed at how gentle their ending had been. She'd accepted his proposal on her birthday and then, in a panic, slept with his cousin and told him immediately. There were some weeks of confusion and pain, and at the time it felt like the most acute emergency of her life, but now she marvels at how gently they dealt with the matter, how little was asked or said.

It was the first great pain for either of them. They hadn't yet opened the door behind strong feeling that lets us through to the black place where we take up weapons, however ancient or redundant. You have to smash your way out of the black place and will do so with whatever comes to hand.

Raif has been trying to let Helen know that he's there now beside her. For a week or two she's filled with joy and then she starts to think that this is not a beginning (so long deferred) but perhaps all there will be. How little she's come to expect.

She looks across the room and sees a man in grief as usual. He has said he's moved on, drawn a line, reconciled himself and is ready. If he really believes that, why does he keep saying it? And why does he look the same? Now and then she catches sight of the person he says he now is – alive, awake, feeling – but none of this is flowing towards her. She is not why.

As she waits for him to come back from the bedroom and explain what he's doing and where he's been, she gives up her generosity and patience. He is not who she thought he was and neither is she. As she steps through the door into the black place, she doesn't know which of them she wants to hurt most: Raif for his failure to love her or herself for insisting that he might. In the black place she sees that he stands behind his wife's death because of what he can then hide. With great sadness, she picks up her weapons.

You come home at midnight, don't explain where you've been, rush off to the bedroom, shut the door and make a call. What's going on?

He is startled by this voice into telling the absolute truth.

I'm trying to find my wife.

For Helen, this is too much. He hasn't moved past anything.

She's dead!

Raif looks at her as if she's pulled off a mask.

But you're right, she says, you're still looking for her. That's why you went to Estonia – to find yourself a new version. You think I don't know?

Know what?

You met someone while you were there.

Yes, I did, but—

You saw her tonight, says Helen. You told me you were seeing a colleague but it was her.

She is a colleague. She's here at a conference.

Is his relationship ending because he had dinner with a woman he hasn't slept with and doesn't even like? He panics.

She's fifty. At least.

And that's supposed to reassure me?

(It had been.)

She's a colleague. We talked about funding and—

But that's not how you met, is it?

No, it isn't.

And she doesn't know you have a girlfriend, does she?

Did he mention Helen? He can't remember.

For fuck's sake, Raif. *You* don't even know you have a girlfriend.

This strikes him as true. Helen is shouting now and the more she says, the further his mind retreats. He does nothing as she packs a bag. When she leaves she says – quietly now – that she isn't angry. He has to stop himself asking what she has to be angry about.

He's alone again – even more so now that Liis's death no longer accompanies him. The sadness for Helen and Raif is that just as she has confronted the force of his loss, and given up competing with it, he has set it aside. He sits there in the sudden space of his life and it feels alright. He wonders why he ever rushed to fill it. He doesn't understand that it isn't really empty. Whatever's been gathering in him since last summer will now take up its place.

He owes Ava an apology and asks her to meet him for coffee. She has a spare half-hour.

I have to give my paper and sit on another panel this afternoon, she says as she sits down.

He doesn't pretend to be interested. Now that there is no expectation and it's clear they won't stay in touch, she's a stranger again. He addresses her more formally.

I'm sorry for my reaction to your news about my wife. It was unfair.

I understand why you're angry. You did not know your wife.

I don't think I wanted to know her. I could have found out more. It's not difficult.

No, it isn't.

But I chose not to.

As if you can live in the dark.

Maybe I found it comforting.

So why not be content to live with her death?

I haven't been. And I've been living with someone. At least I was. She left yesterday.

You seem very calm. Did you not want her?

I wanted her.

You wanted sex with her?

And life. I wanted a life with her. I should do. She's lovely.

What kind of life do you want?

Could you answer that question?

She laughs.

I have feelings I can't feel, he says, and I want to be able to.

And you want some wise but sexy woman to come along and make it happen for you.

Something like that.

Neither of them laugh.

So if it's not the one who's just left, who is it?

Raif is about to speak of things he has long known but in the way we know other planets.

Ava yawns but Raif has gathered himself.

I met someone else, you see, last summer. And I don't think I need her to do anything.

Ava yawns once more.

Another boring story, she says.

He thinks this conversation is a liberation when it's just an opportunity to say things out loud without consequence. But he's enjoying telling the truth and believes (for this day at least) that it's not only possible but liberating to live in truth. The truth is obvious if you're willing to recognise it! He will tell only the truth from now on!

He talks about Iris for the first time.

used, broken, lost

Bringing the girls to stay with her mother should have been a mistake but they're enjoying themselves. They claim Jean's attention so confidently that she gives it. What would that have been like? Iris had barely been able to get Jean to look up from her book or away from her mirror but here she is devoting whole days to trips to the swimming pool, the shopping centre and cinema.

One evening Jean gets boxes of clothes down from the attic and offers the girls her make-up bag. They're sitting in the kitchen. Kate has a gold-and-navy silk scarf knotted at her neck, Lou a cherry-pink one.

Granny's cool, Kate says. She lets us play with her things.

This pleases Jean.

Your mother used to say cool.

You'll get tomato sauce on those scarves, says Iris, but they don't take them off.

Things are there to be played with, says Jean. Used, broken, lost, it doesn't matter. They're only things.

The girls are impressed.

Do you really mean that? asks Lou. People say that but when something does get lost or whatever, it turns out they don't mean it.

Oh, she means it, Iris says.

Jean does not react and Iris, feeling that she's losing control in some way, proposes a walk.

We could watch the sunset from up on the cliff. Anyone want to come?

No one does.

The house is halfway up a hill, on a steep street of Edwardian villas. Iris's childhood memories are filled with the leathery green of rhododendrons, ivy and laurel, and those superfluous turrets and high walls of dark, damp stone that look so promising. The houses behind the walls were always smaller and more drab than these might suggest. Most are now B&Bs and Jean has just announced that she's turning the top floor into a holiday let from the coming summer. The house is a nightmare to heat.

It might rain or it might stay grey for a week. Iris walks up to the cliff, although she's not going to watch the sunset. It's where she came with her friends as a teenager to smoke or drink and walk back and forth. The most exciting thing about the town is the two-hundred-foot drop from the cliff to the sea. The eroded edge has started to fall away and the path is now bordered by low wire. Every few hundred yards there's a cluster of cards and soft toys where another boy (they've all been boys so far) drove his car off the road, across the field and over the edge.

She walks on and on, taking no notice of the cards and toys, the ruined abbey or the piling sky because something has shifted. David's condition has contracted into fact and she has room once again for the idea of Raif. Those months of conversation, that delightful sense of something building. Why hasn't he been in touch? He doesn't know about David so where does he think she's gone? And where is he?

As she crosses one field after another, not bothering to stick to the barely indicated paths, she remembers the couple dancing in The Blue Iris and how, when the man pressed his mouth to the woman's neck, a ripple had passed through Iris herself. The thought now of seeing Raif causes another ripple.

She is on the edge of a large ploughed field when the storm breaks and she turns back towards the gate she came through, only it isn't there. The rain is so heavy that the field turns to mud beneath her and she can't see anything she remembers. Did she come past these trees or those? Why hadn't she paid attention? When did it start to grow dark? The thunder and lightning are overhead and she looks for somewhere to shelter but the hedgerow is dense and will not let her in and so she keeps walking along the edge of the field until she sees car lights and makes her way towards them, pressing through the dense under-growth where she can so that she more or less falls down into a lane that she then follows back to town.

Her mother gives her towels and whisky. Even though Iris has been gone for hours, she's neither curious nor alarmed.

I'm surprised at you getting lost so easily, is all she says as they sit opposite one another by the fire.

I'm not, says Iris and then – because of the cold, the fright, the whisky – she starts to cry.

Jean watches but makes no move to comfort Iris, which becomes a relief as layer after layer of grief rises. Getting lost in the storm (*so easily*) was a sign of how much she needed to give way. She cries as if she's still out there in the dark, in the mud and rain with no one watching, but it is because her mother is there (saying only, occasionally and very quietly, *It's alright*) that she can.

At breakfast Jean asks Lou what she'd like to do and Lou shrugs.

That's just like my mother, says Jean. That shrug. Just like her.

No it's not. It's David, Iris says.

Just like my mother, Jean persists.

Am I just like her, Granny? What was she like?

She was quiet, says Iris. Not like you at all.

They've got similar looks as well.

She was your granny, wasn't she, Mum. What was she like?

I don't really know.

Nonsense, says Jean. You adored your grandmother!

What happened to her?

Lou has asked a question that Iris has felt unable to ask her entire life. *Your grandmother is quiet because something happened to her. She saw a terrible thing.* She stands up and starts to clear the breakfast away, wanting and not wanting to hear what her mother might say.

What happened to her? Jean ponders. She died, didn't she? She got old and she died.

Like you will?

Yes, my sweet. And you too.

Iris watches her daughters receive the clear truth. They finish their cereal, fetch their swimming things and set about the day apparently undiminished.

When they were arranging this visit, Iris assumed that

she would be seeing a lot of her brother. Jason lives nearby and teaches at the school they both attended.

Jason comes to lunch and Iris is surprised to find that the girls remember him well. They play board games with him all afternoon and where Iris would never so much as put her hand on her brother's arms, Kate and Lou scramble over him when he pretends to be asleep on the floor. They hug him.

What are you doing tomorrow? Iris asks him as they sit far apart on the sofa that evening watching the news. We could revisit the haunts of our youth.

Growing up, they'd rarely done anything together.

I'm busy, Jason says. I have things to do.

Jason comes on Saturdays, Jean says. That's why he's here today.

Visit us in London, Iris pleads.

I'm busy, Jason says. And I've seen London. We take a school trip there every year. Why did your husband leave you?

He had a stroke, she says. You come to London? Every year?

The next morning Lou has more questions.

Granny, why did Grandad go away?

Because I asked him to.

Did he get another wife?

No, not that. It was never that.

Couldn't he have come back?

No, my love.

Why not?

I didn't want him.

Iris wishes she could say it like that – *I didn't want him.* She'd like to be as frank as her mother but not as truthful, no. *Mum, why won't you come to the school play? Because that sort of thing bores me. Do you like my haircut? Not really.* Perhaps if she'd been more direct with Raif, they would be something by now. He had reached out and touched her face and what had she done? Asked if she should leave. And he'd said yes. Perhaps it was best that the thing had fizzled out after all.

One evening the girls appear in trailing floral maxi dresses they've taken from the trunk of clothes.

Take a photo! they command.

Your mother liked to have a photo taken when she dressed up too, Jean says.

Show us! Show us!

Oh, I threw all that sort of thing out years ago.

The girls nod as if this is the most reasonable thing they've ever heard.

a switch

Two people say yes and enjoy a time of undescribed connection. They find a reason to talk and perhaps to meet but neither acts. Time passes and the connection fades. When they meet again they've forgotten that this other person had once been such a powerful idea that they might have given up a life to be with them. What had they imagined this person to possess? The switch has been turned off as abruptly as it was turned on. Neither wants to remember how susceptible they once were. It's embarrassing.

Even if these intensities take years to resolve, we can recover from them if they go unnamed. Otherwise we carry them around like a black box, busy with its invisible work.

Many of the objects in the museum's collections explain themselves. The fire is lit here, the steam builds here, the piston lifts, the wheel turns. This lever raises this arm, which presses this button. How does a museum interest its audience in a black box? Even if it were opened, what would they see? The caption on the wall explains the power of this object and so we stop to contemplate a small black box. We believe in it without needing to open it. What else is there to say?

This particular box is a switch that was used in the city's first internet exchange. It was made in 1994 and so is neither new nor old but it is obsolete. Its only function now is to represent one of many steps rapidly taken. It was made in the year of the Superhighway Summit, a year in which the Channel Tunnel opened and there was much talk of nuclear disarmament. The city's drive was towards connection and dialogue, as fast and multi-directional as possible. To connect and connect and connect, never resting or completing, like those who move past one lover to the next, fulfilled at the point of first touch.

blossom

Raif is walking home under a pale-pink sky. It's the time of year when the days seem abruptly extended and the light of eight o'clock is not yet taken for granted. The quieter streets have their cherry trees, crab apples and magnolias now in blossom through vanilla to magenta. Something is softening.

He arrives at his flat, where the jolt of Helen's absence is softened by fresh thoughts of Iris. He does not doubt that she is where he left her – on the bridge in that lemony light. They were about to hold hands. He doesn't want to think about meeting her at the funeral. She saw him with Helen. No wonder she didn't get in touch. (Has he forgotten the three missed calls?) And she said her husband had MS, only she doesn't really think of him as her husband any more. She was saying that for Helen.

Raif opens windows, puts on music and writes to Iris. It's been four months since they were last in touch. He knows now what he is moving towards. Not Helen and not the memory of Liis. It is Iris. He has her in place.

How are you?

It's all he writes and it goes through Iris like a spear. She makes herself wait ten minutes before she replies.

I don't know. You?

In blossom, he writes, and then deletes it and starts again. A lot has happened. Sorry not to have been in touch.

Likewise, she replies.

These brief lines are so appealing. They could only be written by two people sure of their call on the other's attention.

I'd like to see you.

How about next weekend?

Dinner on Saturday?

Sure.

Who says what doesn't matter. They are back walking off the bridge in the lemony light, the people around them no more than murmur and shadow, nothing tugging at or encroaching on or obstructing their delicate becoming.

practical momentum

For Iris, receiving these few words from Raif is as exciting as his fingertips touching her cheek. She experiences such a punch of desire that her body folds. At the same time she's reminded of meeting him with Helen after the funeral and her face burns. She's folding and burning, opening and closing.

Raif has placed Iris in front of Helen, whom he tried to place in front of Liis. This is a form of practical momentum. There is so much to get past in order to love that we must arrange things, including the lover, in as helpful a way as possible.

As we watch Iris and Raif turn towards each other again, we can see all the reasons they've done so. They will never say *I am here because I'm lonely or disappointed. Because I need comfort, sex, to be held, not to fall. Because I'm tired. Because when I was ready I already knew you were a possibility.* They should not be ashamed. These are all aspects of how love becomes possible. They are what creates the unforced space love depends on. Iris and Raif didn't have that space when they were walking off the bridge. They needed something to slow them down and it has.

They should know by now that we never feel one thing at a time. Having accumulated so much, how can we? The tissue of feeling can be prised apart into layers that are easy to define but not to reconcile. So we travel its surface, striving to feel whatever can be called right or good or reasonable.

history

Iris and Raif are about to step out of all that's been happening and meet – for dinner in a restaurant that's borrowed a tall narrow house which, over two centuries, has been divided, boxed in, bricked up, broken open and restored while its value has plummeted and rocketed. In six months' time the developers will move in but meanwhile its dilapidations are recast as virtues: the bare wooden boards of the uneven stairs, the stained plaster walls scattered with islands of old wallpaper.

Iris and Raif are led to a table pressed up against the sill of a wide-open sash window. The air is so still that there's no sense of where inside gives way to outside. Raif fears he might tip into the street so he holds himself with particular care. He appears to Iris as if he's filled with dread.

The food takes an hour to come and while it looks charming – translucent pinks and greens – it tastes muddled. For the first half of that hour neither Iris nor Raif knows what to say. His foot is tapping uncontrollably and she is drinking faster than might be seemly. The people around them look young and at home. While Iris and Raif sit up straight, these others sprawl and wander about. The atmosphere makes Iris feel old and Raif somehow ashamed.

Then the conversation falls open. They look one another in the eye and say what they want to.

Tell me about your girlfriend.

We've split up. As he says it, he tries to recall how it came about.

I had no idea.

Iris flushes but tells herself it's just the wine. She meant to say that she had no idea Helen was his girlfriend. But of course she had.

Her discomfort makes Raif nervous.

Girlfriend is a silly word, don't you think?

Iris looks baffled. He starts again.

I introduced you – last autumn?

(The party where she first saw them together.)

Did you? I can't quite remember.

With that she believes she has recovered her dignity.

I had no idea either, he continues. What you were dealing with.

You mean David? His MS, his infidelities or his stroke?

She sounds as if she's telling a joke but Raif, who has no ear for jokes, hears pain. Before he can think about what he's doing, he has reached across the table and taken her hand. He doesn't let go.

They sit there in silence as if listening to the music that's being played two floors below.

Are you about to ask me to dance?

Yes.

Keeping hold of her hand, he leads her downstairs to the basement club but it's so full that they hover in the corridor, wondering what to do. The beat is too rigid for any kind of dancing they might attempt but Raif is determined. In the end he draws her towards him as if about to waltz and sets off in a slow revolve.

Is he prompted by the memory of the couple they watched dancing in The Blue Iris? Have they haunted him too? His gesture seems all the more powerful to her for being an echo of that moment. It's as if he's repeating something from their slight history.

kissing

What do others make of this shy middle-aged couple dancing in a basement corridor? She is small but stately and he has grace to match. They are serious people, you can tell, who are doing their best to let down their guard. Even so, they have buried their heads.

A group emerge from the club, and Raif and Iris find their way in. A song comes on that she loves and she winds her way into the crowd, trailing one hand behind her, which Raif fails to take. He doesn't follow but she isn't discouraged. Dancing makes her feel as if she's escaped herself and at the same time is more herself than ever. She catches sight of Raif leaning against a wall watching her. His gaze is so new.

He's happy just to stand there watching her dance, which makes her think that she has found someone with whom she can be her true self. Only that phrase has its echoes. *With David I can be my true self. With Adam I can be my true self.* She stops dancing and asks Raif if they can leave.

As soon as they're in the street Raif draws her to him again and they kiss and for that moment there is no qualification or comparison or sense of repetition. Kissing one person is never like kissing another and the first kiss will always be itself – terrible or electrical, awkward or melting. For Iris this kiss has the same certainty as their dancing. For Raif it is something he recognises but has never encountered before. They remain in each other's arms until a couple of boys push past and snigger.

We're too old for this, says Iris.

Raif says exactly what she hopes he will.

No, we're not.

At the entrance to the underground, Iris gathers her courage.

The girls are staying with their aunt.

Can I see you home?

(It's the other side of the city from where he lives.)

Yes, she says. Why not?

The train is crowded and they have to sit opposite each other. Fixed in place by strangers as they move further into the night, they look and look. No wonder they can't stop smiling. But the train comes to a stop in a tunnel and the warmth Iris has been enjoying concentrates into a terrible heat. Her guts curdle and she tastes acid in her mouth. She remembers this.

There had been a flicker on the platform – the same sensation that prompted her to leave the station the day Raif came to see the cloud mirror – but she refused it. She'd been feeling so good, her senses turned up, the so-so food seeming delicious, the wine delicious, the shy dance in the corridor one of the great erotic moments of her life, only now she's stuck on a train with a man she might become trapped with. In a small space she can't get out of.

Raif has his own sources of anxiety and while this is not one of them, he understands. He sees Iris clench her body as if she's about to burst out of herself. Her eyes are shut, her hands are gripping her dress, her legs are drawn in. She wants to make herself into a knot but must do this discreetly as the worst fear is that people will notice. They will see what she contains. Nothing. Her greatest fear is that at her core there is nothing. Was that her grandmother's fear too?

He wills her to open her eyes and when she does, he holds her gaze. She lets the fear and horror pass out of herself because he is inviting her to share it with him. He doesn't speak or smile or reach out but he holds her. She tries not to think about the fact that David rescued her on a train in a tunnel too. Over the years her panic occasionally returned, something David took as an insult. Hadn't he cured her? If she became anxious he would detach himself and become just another stranger, a person she ought to protect from such mess.

The train starts to move and just like that, everything is alright. Perhaps it's not the closed door or the tunnel that frightens her but the idea of nothing moving, of not moving, of being unmoved. At the next station Raif guides her out of the train and into a cab. He holds her all the way home and follows her in, at which point she starts to panic again.

I think I have a migraine coming.

What do you need?

I'll take my pills, some water, get some sleep. I'll be fine.

Raif has noticed that she's shaking.

Why don't you get into bed? I'll bring you some water.

She goes up, wondering why she lied.

He knocks on the door.

I thought something warm might be better so I made

honey and lemon. Let me know if it needs adjusting.

Raif's modest care touches her. If David had done such a thing, he would present it with a flourish and demand applause. She would have to declare it perfect and he'd be angry when she did not directly recover.

Raif closes the door and goes to the bathroom. Like the rest of the house, it's too small for what it must contain but whereas every other room he's seen is tightly ordered, this one is in chaos. There are two dresses thrown over the side of the bath: black (too wintry, Iris had thought) and white (she's tired and would look washed out). There's a tangle of tights on the floor and a pair of glossy high heels that he cannot imagine her wearing – though the thought of her doing so stays with him. On the shelf beneath the mirror is a heap of cosmetics. He treads on a hairbrush and spots a puddle of the grey nail polish she's wearing congealed on the side of the bath.

Wanting to do something for her, he puts the lids on her lipstick and creams, and untangles the tights and arranges them on a chair beneath which he places the shoes. He puts the hairbrush in the bathroom cupboard, trying not to scan the shelves. This unexpected access to knowledge of her feels like a dangerous gift.

What is it she needs? She looked at ease on the dance floor, which he had not expected. And her dancing was full of skilful intricacies: the tilt of her head, the roll of her hip, her wrist angled just so. But then there was the sudden agony she felt when the train stopped and how hard she worked to control it.

He wonders if she's asleep and if he should leave and

what is a migraine exactly? He goes downstairs, sits on the sofa and looks about him. There are folders stacked on a narrow desk. For want of something to do, he looks at them. There is one labelled Work and another labelled House, a third, The Girls. The fourth says David. Raif thinks of himself as the kind of person who would never open such a folder but he can't ask her about David, who although still alive is so out of reach that he occupies the same realm as Liis. Raif opens the folder. It's empty.

Upstairs, Iris is trying to have a migraine or at least to sleep. She's uneasy about pretending to be ill but she wants so much to leave her panic in the past and not have it contaminate this next beginning. She pictures Raif opening cupboards and looking through drawers, and is ashamed of this thought, and then relieved when she hears the front door open. He has had the good sense to leave without saying goodbye.

daylight

The next morning Iris wakes up feeling many things. She's proud of the dancing, astonished by the kissing and horrified by her panic on the train. She gave in to herself so easily. And suggested he come home with her when she hadn't meant it. Or had she? Getting ready to meet Raif, she had prepared for sex while telling herself that they were just going to have dinner. She put on music loud enough to prompt the neighbours to bang on the wall, shaved her legs, oiled her skin and put a lot of thought into her underwear. Desire and panic have brought her back to her body, which she's done her best not to think about for years. They seem like one feeling and were she to follow them to their source, she might discover that they are. She has anyway a sense of imminent turbulence as her forties tip into her fifties.

When she sees the tidied bathroom, her dresses and shoes, she's embarrassed and then touched. Raif had been so tactful (she hasn't retained anything he said) and he behaved as if her migraine (panic) were perfectly reasonable.

He phones mid-morning.

I was worried about you.

I'm fine.

Your migraine?

The pills saw it off.

I'll come to see you this afternoon.

Raif is speaking with firmness. His modesty means that he is hesitant but also resilient. And this morning he feels as potent as he did when he crossed the room to speak to Liis for the first time. He doesn't think of Liis when he looks at Iris but it is true that he has been drawn to another calm surface when what really attracts him lies beneath. But Iris is not a frozen lake. She's a dry structure, her layers formed under pressure and difficult to erode. Raif is bemused, frightened, moved and aroused; perturbed by her invisible children, envious of her sick husband and determined to secure himself in relation to her somehow.

He arrives at two o'clock, bringing a bunch of pale irises in bud. She pretends he's the first man to do this because David (or Adam) would have been upset if she had not. Raif sees through her badly performed surprise and laughs.

I can't be the first person to have given you irises.

You're not.

He doesn't mind but wonders if he ought to.

She makes tea and they sit opposite one another. What now? Iris feels as if she's trying to open a tightly folded piece of paper.

I asked you to come home with me and then—

Raif almost drops his cup.

No, no, I suggested I see you home.

We meant the same thing, though.

She sounds calm but looks past him.

On the train, I panicked. It wasn't a migraine. I told myself it was but it wasn't.

There's no need to explain.

I wasn't unwell. I was panicking.

You don't like the underground?

It's difficult. Yes.

She tells herself she is claustrophobic, the layer of explanation at which her mind sensibly stops. She will not ask why the panic always starts when she dares to feel fully alive and does not know that this sensation is fullness and not emptiness – it is everything rather than nothing. He knows what she's going to say – that this is too sudden or too soon – but what she says is

I scared myself. How much I wanted—

He quickens, anticipating the word *you*. *How much I wanted you.*

How much I wanted to—

They are caught in a slab of light. No music, just teacups and dust and weary faces. He tries to think of something to say that will return them to the night before.

How much you wanted to dance?

No, she says, still looking past him. How much I wanted to fuck.

She says it to prove it to herself and it works. Her body is determined. Raif makes a small sound, less than breathing out, as he locks into this desire. He builds no sentences, forms no thoughts.

Iris starts to unbutton her dress, which is the one she wore the night before. He counts the buttons – twelve. She undoes six and stretches herself in the armchair so that the dress falls away. He can trace one side of her from shoulder to breast and the length of one thigh.

She sits back. Her body requires a familiar arrangement, the one established when she and David first met. Will he know not to move towards her?

Raif wonders if he should undress too. It doesn't worry him to be naked. He's never had much expectation of his body. But he does nothing. Iris will determine what happens next because he, too, is following familiar steps. He looked to Liis for direction. The more obliquely it was given, the more it excited him to interpret what was required.

But this is not some candlelit bedsit or corporate flat. They are two middle-aged people trying to persuade themselves into sex on a Sunday afternoon. What now? Iris gets up and leaves the room.

Raif decides that he is being invited to go and find her. She has drawn the curtains in the bedroom and is naked now but under the covers and turned towards the wall. He takes off his clothes. As soon as he's beside her, she pushes his hand from her waist to between her legs. There is the flare of first touch but what then?

He's stroking her vaguely, wondering how she prefers this to be done. He knows that there isn't one way to do anything. *Each woman is different*, he reminds himself. *I must learn about this woman.* He wants to have her known so that he won't have to feel so uncertain again. It hasn't occurred to him that a body can be unlocked in different ways at different times and that someone's desire is a puzzle their lover might go on solving.

When Raif met Helen he was deep in his grief. His world turned inwards and so when they fucked he went towards memory and fantasy and barely noticed her. He didn't wonder whether the sex was good because he didn't care. Now he feels more than he has in a long time and it scares him. He worries that he's being clumsy and that he's not staying hard. Iris thinks he's being sensitive. His hesitation is matched by her own because her body seems not to know how to open. She wants this to be fear but knows it might be age. A response she has taken for granted is no longer there: not out of reach or misfiring in some way, just not there.

As soon as it becomes clear that they're not going to have sex after all, they settle back into themselves. Raif draws Iris towards him and puts his head against hers while his hand lightly, solemnly, strokes the hair back from her forehead. She realises that she's lost all expectation of tenderness and this makes her cry.

Raif's mouth is against her ear so that she feels rather than hears the words.

It's alright, my love. It's alright.

These tiny vibrations carry their meaning into her heart and she believes him. *It's alright.*

Raif could not explain to Ava what it is about Iris that draws him. He doesn't want to impress her or rescue her or even enchant her, he wants to listen.

They lie for some time as if asleep and then Iris, being thorough, tries to explain.

It's probably because it's been a while since . . . she begins.

Since you and your husband?

Yes.

A crack runs through this. Just after David moved out she bumped into Martin at another party. This time there were no lost keys. Nor were there spouses. Martin and his wife had decided to try a separation. Iris contrived to leave at the same time as Martin and he offered her a lift. She invited him in and they drank a bottle of wine. When she stood up he pulled her onto his lap, her body instantly agreeing as he shoved himself inside her. It lasted a couple of minutes and she saw him to the door as soon as he'd tucked in his shirt. They'd completed the evening they started all those years ago and would be indifferent to one another from then on.

What about you? she asks Raif. Was Helen the first person after your wife died?

Yes, he says, and he believes himself.

It is five o'clock on a Sunday afternoon in May. A blunt light persists at the window but Raif and Iris prefer to remain beyond its reach.

a museum

The girls are dropped off by their aunt at seven. The windows are wide open and their mother is listening to music. Is this good or bad? She's jolly and attentive and asks lots of questions but doesn't wait for an answer. Something is pulling her away and so they follow her around.

Mum, do you think Dad would like a birthday card?

Why are you putting everything on the floor?

Or should we record a message. Like a video he can watch?

You need to put it all back.

Would they show it to him?

Would you?

Don't pile those up. You'll break them.

Would he listen?

Dad gave you that.

You're not listening, Mum.

Are you listening, Mum?

Mum?

Every response is an effort. She's drawn inwards towards what happened that afternoon, which was moving, alarming, mortifying and somehow so lovely that she keeps thinking she's going to cry. *It's alright, my love. It's alright.*

Mum. You're not listening. Mum.

Raif sends a message that evening. *Thinking of you.*

Hope you're alright. When it arrives Iris is arguing with Lou and doesn't hear her phone.

When the girls come down to say goodnight she is out in the garden, smoking. For a second she sees them as their actual selves. Lou's body is preparing to stretch and round. She looks watery and shadowed. Not even thirteen, Iris thinks.

You need new pyjamas, she says as she walks back into the house.

Lou has taken to looking at the floor when she speaks, as if her head has become too heavy.

I like these ones.

Her voice is heavy with something too.

The trousers come halfway down Lou's shins and she's wearing a T-shirt under the jacket as she can no longer do it up. How could Iris not have noticed?

You've grown.

I haven't.

We won't, adds Kate.

Iris will buy new pyjamas – for them both so as to be fair – and they'll say thank you, put them in a drawer and wear the old ones. She can no longer make them do otherwise.

At midnight Iris finds her phone. She writes four different responses to Raif's message before sending the one that says *Fine, thank you. You?* Raif adjusts himself. He waits a day before writing again and so she waits two. A week passes in which they are barely in touch. Iris wonders when he actually finished with Helen. Raif is wondering this too.

In the morning Lou beckons Kate over to the cupboard.

I've got something else for the museum.

Lou holds out the gold-and-topaz tiepin.

It's David's.

How do you know it's David's?

It was pinned to the lining of one of his jackets.

Why would you pin something on the inside of your jacket?

Perhaps he didn't want anyone to know he was wearing it.

How come you found it?

I was looking for something. Nothing. I dunno. Dad.

Kate doesn't ask Lou to explain. She's a steady child who has a strong sense of what she doesn't want to know. Her reaction to all this upheaval has been to move as firmly through each day as she can. Lou has noticed this and admires it in her.

the wonder box

The first time Iris took the girls to the museum, she showed them the wonder box. They were only little and it was, after all, a kind of toy. But it was behind glass and they couldn't understand why they weren't allowed to play with it, why they were supposed to just stand there and look.

The wonder box was invented in the 1920s by the pioneering child psychologist Margaret Lowenfeld. It contains thirty-two toys including a polar bear, a palm tree, soldiers, a snowman, a nurse and pram, a well, and a horse and cart. The box itself is more of a tray, half-filled with sand. Children who couldn't find the words to convey what they needed to were able to invent a world and therefore a story that reflected their own.

These we arrange and rearrange in various ways . . . making a world of them. In doing so we have found out all sorts of pleasant facts, and also many undesirable possibilities.

It might seem more useful to offer children paper, crayons or clay so that they could build a world out of whatever came to mind. Why impose a pram and a polar bear? Perhaps because the details of specific objects offer something ready made. The child is not alone in empty space with their story. There's something already there, things that they can play with and perhaps have a conversation with too.

We then dress our islands, objecting strongly to too close a scrutiny of our proceedings until we have done.

The toys make no sense as a group and so the child is free to invent the laws of this other world. It is on their scale and within their control. They can take their time in building it and be sure that it's strong enough for what they need it to demonstrate and contain.

what if she falls?

Ashley is driving Raif from the station to his mother's house. When he got off the train she almost didn't recognise him. He stood out.

What's happened to you, then? she asks as soon as they get into the car.

Raif has all the freshness of feeling that we take for being in love but he cannot trust it.

I'm worried, he says.

About your mother? I'm not surprised.

He hasn't visited for three weeks.

You're making me even more worried.

You should be.

She sounds fine whenever we speak.

Of course she does. She thinks she is.

Raif has always been close to his mother and has found her easy to love, so why won't he face this? Perhaps because he feels as helpless as he did standing beside his father's body or watching Liis die. All he can do is refuse what's happening. He can't protect his mother any other way.

What he finds is that Bridget has started to empty space in herself. She has a fixed expression of benign wonder and moves in a slow dance from room to room.

What if you fall? he asks and she laughs.

She spends her days wandering the lands of her own

home, startled by a picture or transfixed by a bowl, the pattern in the carpet, dust in the air. The less she remembers, the brighter it all becomes.

Raif is there today to meet a social worker who wants to reassess Bridget's needs.

You want a heat sensor above the cooker. Alarms on the front and back doors. Weren't you supposed to have those put in already? Rails in the bathroom and an emergency cord. Why isn't she wearing her personal alarm?

She takes it off, says Raif.

Lucky there are no stairs. Unusual windows. Very large. Is that safety glass? The carer will come in a second time each day. But you need to organise the shopping. Does your mother have any savings?

What if she falls? Raif asks.

Is your mother an owner-occupier?

I think you should leave, Bridget says.

Raif leaps to apologise.

I'm sorry, she doesn't mean to—

You, his mother says, pointing at Raif. I think you should leave.

But I'm—

Who are you?

She turns to the social worker.

I want him to leave.

And she starts to shout.

Make him go away!

Raif waits in the kitchen. The social worker suggests that he stays elsewhere tonight. She is organising someone to come by that evening to settle Bridget and give her a meal. Sometimes family members become the focus of irrational fears. It means nothing.

All three triplets come to pick him up. Emily drives, and Ashley and Jessica surround him.

She doesn't mean it but you should try to respect her wishes.

Stay with us and go back in the morning.

Have you got power of attorney?

They take him to their parents' house, where everyone crowds round the kitchen table. The house isn't big enough for three children, let alone three grown-up daughters, but they flow round one another as they do in conversation, while their parents sit happily in the middle of it all. Neil, too, is struck by some difference in Raif.

So who's turned the lights on?

Raif doesn't realise that Neil is talking to him. Sorcha nudges her husband.

Leave the boy alone!

The boy? one or two of the triplets say.

He's right, though.

Whoever she is, says Neil, I hope she's not so —

Not like —

She isn't, is she?

Raif hesitates. Do they mean Liis or Helen? The triplets make a point of never mentioning Helen. He says nothing, knowing that the conversation will move on.

He sleeps in one of the two rooms the triplets use, which is a swirl of clothes, books, earrings, tampons, phones, hair straighteners, photos, birthday cards, credit cards, exam papers. It's as if they neither throw anything away nor make any effort to keep it. They share everything. If nothing is precious or private, you can always find what you need.

In the morning Sorcha announces that she's going to drive to the downs for a walk and invites Raif to come along. As they arrive, a car pulls up beside them and a man gets out. He looks a little like Neil but he's taller, more elegant, more silvery, and he has an extreme, unfading smile.

This is my friend Alan, Sorcha says. And this is my nephew, Raif.

I've heard all about you, says Alan. What a beautiful day!

It is damp and dull. Alan leads them up a path on which two but not three can comfortably walk side by side. Sorcha falls in with Raif and asks him how he thinks his mother is.

Look! shouts Alan. Bird's-foot trefoil!

Sorcha hurries over, intoning the name, and takes out her phone to photograph a clump of yellow flowers. They walk on and a few minutes later Alan stops abruptly and whispers that he can see a butterfly.

It looks like a green hairstreak!

A green hairstreak, Sorcha murmurs, and photographs the sprig of leaves at which Alan is pointing.

Raif's phone rings. It's his mother. He says that he's on a walk with Sorcha and will be over soon and not to make any lunch, he will do that. While he's talking, Sorcha and Alan walk on ahead. She has taken his arm. (What if she falls?) Raif makes sure that he lags a little behind, thinking it only polite. They continue on, Alan pointing out a flower, a herb, a feather, and Sorcha photographing whatever he names.

It's sweet, isn't it? This friendship or whatever it is. Sorcha has found something she's been missing and it does no harm. Raif doesn't realise that this is exactly what her husband has been telling himself for years: *they're friends, they go for walks, it's nothing.*

They come to the top. Raif has known this view all his life and still finds it exhilarating to see the downs rippling into the distance. The sun breaks through and splashes across the fields and he turns to his aunt, about to shout *Look!* but she's trying to hear what Alan has just heard.

Shh, listen – a corn bunting, perhaps?

Jessica drives him back to his mother's house.

How was your walk?

Great, says Raif. We saw a green hairstreak. At least, Alan did.

Alan.

She says the name with a finalising laugh and Raif makes a note not to mention Alan again. When they pull up outside Bridget's house, Jessica has something she wants to say.

You know, I never liked Liis.

Raif is startled. No one has ever criticised Liis.

You didn't know her, he says.

I mean, I didn't like how she was. With you. How you felt.

How do you know what I felt?

It was obvious. You felt small.

I am small. Besides which, you were a child when we got married.

You still looked small.

He had felt small, it was true, in his life with Liis. He'd had so little effect.

Is Jessica's dislike of Liis insight or hindsight? Either way, Raif has been given permission to feel differently about his dead wife. When his aunt comes by that afternoon, Raif asks what she thought of Liis, honestly.

Honestly? I found her a bit boring.

Liis has always had only powerful traits – absoluteness, detachment, reticence – which he fashioned out of her opacity. Perhaps she had been quite ordinary.

where certainty lies

On the train home Raif decides that he's drifting. He's been carried towards Iris, away and now back. They could have passed each other by, only now they've been brought to the start of something and they need to act. Their night out was a turning point but they are close to drifting again. He has to act.

When he contemplates her body, it's the moment of dancing in the corridor that comes to mind rather than the afternoon in bed when they started to undress and didn't know what to do. Iris was remarkable in the way she took charge but there's been nothing of that Iris in her messages since.

Helen is sitting at the kitchen table packing crockery. He wonders if they had an arrangement that he's forgotten. He bends to kiss her but she turns away so that he kisses the top of her head, breathing in a scent that brings back the slow trail of her hair across his skin, her definite way of moving when naked, her definite hands and definite mouth. As he fusses with the kettle and repeatedly offers biscuits, he's arguing with his body, which is recalling things about this woman that his mind doesn't want to allow. Perhaps she'd only gone away for a few days and has now come home. But she's sitting there wrapping plates.

I knew you'd probably be at your mother's, she says, so I thought it would be a good time to collect my things.

So they have split up. He calms down.

You didn't let me know you were coming, he says, trying to sound unperturbed.

No, I didn't. You look better.

I don't know that I am but yes, maybe.

Since they met, Helen has been flowing towards him. Now she is quite still. He's beginning to understand that he has not treated her well.

She gets up and walks into the bedroom. Raif follows because he doesn't know what else to do and watches as she pulls down her suitcase from the top of the wardrobe and starts throwing in clothes. Shoes, books, cosmetics, tools, a radio – she bundles them all into the case as if she can't wait to get out of there.

Do you want to talk? he asks, although the idea horrifies him.

Helen starts to talk.

The thing is, your broken heart made you interesting.

It's not broken any more.

Maybe not but this is. Or you are.

She moves past him and on to the bathroom, where she shoves jars, brushes and compacts from a shelf into a bag. He'd emptied the cabinet of pills and the drawers of Liis's clothes when he got back from Estonia but he hadn't invited Helen to use the space.

Raif watches as she clears the place of herself with great sweeps of her hands. How tall she is, how elegant and resilient! How confusing.

It won't work, he blurts.

It's the line he's been rehearsing for weeks and has only managed to say now that it's no longer required.

Helen laughs as if it hurts her to do so.

It never did. I had to be us – if there ever was an us – on my own.

She's finished packing. He's shocked by how quickly all trace of her is gone. He's going to be on his own again with the beige surfaces. But Helen is still there, leaning against the wall. His eyes are drawn to the push of her gorgeous hips.

When you offered me a place to stay, you behaved like I'd moved in on you for life.

You didn't mean to stay?

She had hoped she might.

We were hardly ready for that, she says, and anyway it was like being around a ghost.

Of my wife?

No. You. You were the ghost.

He's about to offer to help her with her boxes but there's more.

I met someone, she says, and they reminded me.

Reminded you of what?

He feels obliged to ask but is not at all sure he wants to know. She doesn't reply.

Someone sat down beside her and, like Raif and Iris walking through the doorway at the museum, Helen and this person said yes. She'd gone out into the city and found where certainty lies – in the moment when the yes is said. Nothing is as sure. In the enchantment that will follow, she will become another version of herself. Just as Raif is more present with Iris and Iris is more open with him, Helen will be more powerful this time. Her next lover will flow towards her.

The next version of ourselves is not necessarily an improvement. Raif became detached, Helen tentative, David lied and Iris built walls. But we proceed in the hope that it can be. We look to love as a way of transforming ourselves and so blame our lover if we don't like who we become.

Helen is still talking.

I'd forgotten that it's possible to be certain. Not that it'll become something but that it's there. And that it's to do with me, who I am, me in particular. Not just what the other person needs.

(What else is love but convincing someone that it can only be them?)

Helen has been redirected. Although she's looking at Raif, she's making no attempt to take him in. He might be a passing cloud in which she can't be bothered to look for a shape.

You seem surprised, she says.

No. Just a bit. Yes.

The first thing I was taught to do as an actor was to give up my dignity. It's dangerous. But it makes so much possible.

Why are you telling me this?

She could be about to explain him to himself, the Raif she has known, but she's no longer that interested.

I don't know, she says.

She'll come back to collect the rest of her things another day and will be in touch. She offers him his key but he tells her to keep it for now.

A few days later Helen sends a message.

I was the ladder out of your grief.

In which case she brought him back to the surface and there was Iris waiting to greet him. Raif should feel bad about this but he doesn't because what has arisen with Iris seems to have no connection to anything else. As yet there is nothing about it that seems either familiar or repeated. And he is able to be there when he's with Iris – properly there. Why, he has no idea. He replies to Helen, thanking her for her insight. He tries to agree with what she says but feels that the reason for their failure is more opaque. Or that there isn't one.

the shape it takes

Iris, too, is wondering at herself. She actually said that she wanted to fuck. She managed to translate her fear into courage and she decides that Raif made this possible. Otherwise she is the more cautious one, partly because of how love surrounds her. The circle that Adam drew around her and then stepped into. How long it took for the idea of stepping out of it to occur. Adam had been a difficult, and therefore a great, love. This is her version and has become her memory. How he smashed his way into her life cannot be held in words and so lies behind a wall.

Who was she? For years, the woman David described: first a goddess, then mysteriously layered and then a series of walls. Only now these ideas are loosening. David had drawn a circle too. Or he hadn't. Maybe Adam hadn't either. Maybe that's what she does every time: draws a circle and then convinces herself that she can't step out of it. Perhaps it's about to happen again. But this man isn't like the others. He's a number of quieter things, not energetic or shining but impressive in ways that she, for some reason, is able to bring out.

The shape love takes depends on what we need it for. It might be to simplify a landscape or to furnish an emptiness, to give our lives more detail or less. For Iris it's the drawing of a circle. For Raif it's the forming of a surface. Whatever it is, we do it ourselves and each time believe it different and the gift of the one we now love.

a strengthening

When they meet again they hesitate once more. They're having lunch on a Saturday while the girls are with friends. Iris is twenty minutes late.

I've got two hours, she says as she sits down. More like an hour and a half.

Raif has already ordered a bottle of wine but Iris says no, she isn't drinking.

Is everything alright?

Yes. No. I had an argument with Lou just before I came out.

What about?

She wants to get her ears pierced.

Iris has shown him pictures of the girls. He can't remember their ages but would have said they were about fourteen and sixteen.

And you think she's too young?

Her sister doesn't want to get hers done.

So if Katie—

Kate.

Sorry. If Kate wanted to do it as well, you'd be more convinced?

One with pierced ears and the other not?

I don't understand what the issue is.

You think I should let them?

That's up to you.

Iris catches up with herself.

It's me, isn't it? I find the idea of them choosing not to look like one another really upsetting.

You do?

Absorbed by this insight, Iris talks about the girls for the rest of lunch – how Lou has started to wait till Kate's dressed and then wears something as different as possible. How they've rearranged their room so that they can't see each other when in bed. How often now she finds one of them alone. Raif tries to be interested but he doesn't understand. They're sisters, that's all. They're growing up.

Iris looks at her watch.

Christ, it's already three. I have to go. Thank you, it's been lovely and you've been . . . Thank you. You really helped.

For Raif this meeting has fallen flat. Iris was late and talked about her children and he hadn't known what to say. But apparently he has helped her and when he reminds himself of this, he feels proud and useful. And with this comes a strengthening of his need for her.

the glamour of the object

The line drawn between Iris and Raif holds across the city as they move through their separate days. Anchored in one another, they are more sure of themselves. People notice them. Students who find themselves alone with Raif in his office stutter and blush. A young man strikes up a conversation with Iris in the museum and asks for her number. She offers him her card and he laughs – not that number. More than once she looks up – in a meeting, on a train – to find someone looking at her with the blank gaze that is the body saying yes.

She and Raif speak each night but it is in their messages, several a day, that they are building something. They're both quick to pick up what might become emblematic. He asks which is her favourite object in the collections and she sends him a picture of a tiny bronze skeleton. It immediately takes up its place alongside the cloud mirror, the merman, her falling down the steps, the walk across the bridge, the dance in the corridor in what is not yet a life but already a story.

Iris is in no hurry to make him a full part of her life. Something reminds her of the early days with Adam in the graveyard and it's true that they come and go from their relationship as if it were a walled garden. *That wasn't real*, she thinks. *This isn't real*. But Raif has his own hesitations and so is untroubled by hers. They set themselves at an equal distance. They limit what they share and continue to shine.

Their meetings depend upon the girls, David, and Raif's mother. One night Iris suggests to Raif that they go back to his flat but he didn't wash up or make the bed before leaving so he finds a way to say no. They stick to meeting in the centre of the city, where so much is designed to carry love along.

Iris continues to study herself. She thinks she's fading just as she has been resensitised. She's besotted with colour, scent, texture and taste. The sky, the river, the objects in her hands, move her. For Raif, this new love is a form of momentum. He takes small steps – talking to his doctor about cutting down his medication, painting one wall of the flat bright white – and thinks of each as decisive.

a skeleton

We hold onto the stuff of the body, invest it with magic and use it to cure or kill. The museum owns hundreds of such instruments and amulets, though they have been removed from view. There are the shrunken heads, of course, but also necklaces of bones painted in red ochre, mourning ornaments of hair wrapped in clay, a wooden doll with human hair that a girl carried on her back to show that she was ready for marriage.

Sometimes the human and animal have been merged in a doubling of strength: the skull of a woman covered in the skin of an antelope, ceremonial shoes made of feathers compacted with human hair and blood, a jawbone tip to an iron spear with a rhinoceros-horn handle.

There is a tooth used to ward off toothache and a tooth said to be the tooth of a king, a glass jar of human dust, a square of skin from the neck of a man hanged for forgery that shows the mark of the rope, excised tattoos, dried brains and dissected blood vessels, freeze-dried plasma, inscribed skulls, drilled skulls, bones made into bowls and flutes. If only our bodies felt this potent and adaptable when we were alive.

Nothing makes us feel more alive than being reminded of our death. This bronze skeleton, a little over four inches high, is 2,500 years old yet her purpose is to remind us of how little time we have. She is a memento mori handed out at Roman feasts. Carefully constructed, with articulated limbs, she has been rearranged. Her left arm is missing because it's been used to replace her right leg. This makes her appear more human than less so. She reminds us not only of our ending but the extent to which we rearrange ourselves in order to persist.

a provocation

Raif has to cancel seeing Iris yet again because his mother rings at four a.m. to ask why he hasn't arrived. *Lunch is getting cold.* He gets dressed and calls a cab, meaning to catch the first train, but then it strikes him that there's little point. If she sets the house on fire the alarm will go off. If she's in trouble the neighbours or carers will find out before he does. He can't give up his job and go to live with her and she would not countenance leaving her home. So that's that.

Only he wakes most nights from a dream of his mother falling, not in the bath or on the stairs but falling unendingly past him, just beyond reach. So he gets on the train and goes down that evening just to check.

The second time he cancels because Ashley has had her phone stolen by a boy on a motorbike who pulled her over as he grabbed it and she's split open her chin. Raif takes her to hospital and by the time she's discharged, both her sisters have arrived and all three come back to stay.

When they do manage to meet, for coffee, Raif tells Iris this story and shows her a picture of the triplets on his phone. As she takes it from his hand her thumb swipes the screen, pictures flick by and she's looking at a woman wearing a silver coat.

That's not them, he says, snatching his phone back.

Clearly. But she looks interesting.

She's Estonian, like my wife.

I see.

She knew her . . . of her . . .

A question starts to form, though Iris will not ask it. There's a version of herself that she has discarded: Iris of the Many Eyes – always seeing deception and secrets where, David insisted, there were none. She knows that these questions do no good and that she cannot stand to hear herself ask them. But Raif snatched back his phone.

She looks pleased, says Iris, that you wanted a photo.

Does she?

At least you met someone who knew your wife.

He wants so much not to lie.

She told me things about Liis's childhood, her family, that Liis never did.

It is Iris who has the strongest sense of what's at stake. She can either push Raif into a smaller and smaller corner or she can trust that whoever this woman is, she's not important now. If she is, Iris will find out soon enough.

Don't tell me her name, she says, and takes his hand so as to change the subject.

Raif raises her hand to his mouth and kisses it. But he can see that for Iris, Ava remains a provocation. Why didn't he just explain?

I'm afraid I'll have to go in a minute, he says.

(Perhaps this too is a lie? Iris wants so much not to have thought this.)

They sit there in silence, two small middle-aged people holding hands in a busy cafe at eleven o'clock on a Friday morning. It would be touching were it not for the fact that they seem unable to move.

fucking

The river pulls back from its banks in strong tides that churn its bed. There are places along its winding length where what's drawn from the mud lingers. A million fragments of ordinary life – clay pipes, beer bottles, buttons and soup bowls – are cast up. They've been in the river for hundreds of years, some thousands, but unless you take them now, they will return to the flow and be carried out to the river mouth and you will never see them again.

Iris wakes early. There is a message from Raif sent at four a.m.: *I should have been clearer. I can explain*, and another at six: *Call me when you wake up*, but she doesn't. It's a late-summer morning without plans or exigencies. The girls are away for a week with their grandparents and although the house is full of things that need doing, she decides to go for a walk. She sets out north through the park and turns east along the river. Maps suggest that you can follow a single path along the riverside. It's something of which the city is proud. But the reality, as Iris finds, is that developments, sold on their views, block the path with overdesigned fences and gates. It is not possible to follow the water's edge without being met by these hostilities.

Iris walks fast, as if she's trying to catch up with something. She's impressed by how much progress she makes despite the detours she follows into back alleys and car parks. But where is she going? When she left her house she was agitated by the woman's photo and Raif's unstraightforward response. By the time she reaches the river she's scared. There are things she has felt that she never wants to feel again.

Maybe her reaction has been out of all proportion to his small faltering lie. But they've established the start of something and she'd anticipated a calm while they gently found their feet. Now one uncertainty is giving way to another. This thing with Raif was worth nothing if it dragged all this behind it.

She climbs the steps onto the bridge that will lead her to Raif, and the sharp pain she's been trying to walk away from shifts its emphasis from fear to feeling. *I want this. It will already hurt me to lose it.* She makes her way between the new towers and the old, looking and not looking for where Raif lives. She has his address memorised and pinpointed on the map on her phone but when she sees the corner of his street she doesn't hesitate to walk straight past it.

Raif has been berating himself. The tension that sprang up in the cafe was familiar: whether to say something or not. After all, he'd spent all that time choosing what to show of himself to Helen and trying to understand the rules when with Liis. Until now he has shown Iris whatever arose. He could have explained that taking Ava's photo was just a way of being polite. This wouldn't be entirely true but it is what he believes now.

He sent his messages at four and at six, and he waited. By ten, the possibility that he's lost her stabs at his heart. He should have called her but he's become so cautious. The steps he has been able to take have been so small. He wants to go straight round to see her, to turn up on her doorstep as a demonstration of who he really is, but remembers that Rosa is back and they've arranged to have a cup of coffee.

Iris is crossing the bridge to the north just as Raif gets on a bus heading west. They'll never meet each other like this. But they've each glimpsed the loss of the other and it has spurred them on.

Rosa and Raif promised to write while she was away but neither got round to it. She's back now and when she walks into the cafe he's incredibly pleased to see her. He needs to talk. Their conversation moves from the islands Rosa was visiting to his mother's illness, the lack of students, the fee increases and the cuts, but this is not what he needs to talk about. Only he can't bring himself to raise the subject. Eventually she does.

Are you still with the girlfriend you never told me about?

No.

But you look happy. Is there someone new?

Her name's Iris.

Rosa sits back. She's looking incredibly pleased with herself.

I think I know who she is.

Did someone tell you?

No, I saw you with her.

When?

At the museum last summer. The small woman in the big dress. You walked in at the same time, side by side, as if you were together. You couldn't stop looking at her. And she was looking too. In the end you just made your way towards each other.

We had a conversation. That was all.

Yes, but I watched you talking.

That's amazing, he says.

Rosa has no particular insight. Anyone could have seen what she did – two people saying yes. But for Raif it's as if something has been tested and proved.

Halfway home, Iris gets a message from Raif suggesting that he come over that evening. He turns up with food, flowers and wine. She lights candles even though it won't get dark for at least an hour. They sit down opposite each other at the laden table but barely eat and cannot think what to say.

My friend Rosa, my colleague, she's been away. We had coffee this morning.

Is this the point where we tell each other about our day?

Of course not. It's just she said something about us. About when we met that night at the museum. She saw us together and she knew.

Knew what?

That something would happen. That we would be this.

His heart has made its declaration.

Iris takes some time to decide on her words.

I'd rather we said it for ourselves than waited to be told.

She sees his disappointment and realises he thought he was passing on a blessing.

But yes, she says. We are this.

She gets up and goes to the open door, where she lights a cigarette, turning away from Raif so he can't see that her hands are shaking. There is something in her movement that is so wonderfully familiar. If he thinks hard enough he might remember that when they walked through the doorway in the museum they stopped simultaneously to scan the room and he turned towards her just as she caught sight of someone else and turned away – just as she had when they'd finally spoken and again as they lay in bed that Sunday afternoon.

Iris is willing him to come towards her, to touch her, and eventually he does. The tips of his fingers trace the back of her broad sunburnt shoulder and his mouth skims the nape of her neck where her hair has just been cropped. He wants to fill his hands with her breasts, her belly, any part of her. He wants to hold her and be deep inside her and to make her feel everything he can. He is kissing her neck, her shoulders and her back as he starts to unzip her dress. She turns and from barely touching they press so hard against each other that they almost fall down. There will not be another game of sitting and looking, and they will not have sex on a bed of weeds and concrete or up against the warped kitchen counter. They go upstairs.

They don't get undressed or wait for directions. They drop onto the bed and pull at each other's clothes, undoing enough that he can find his way inside her. They aren't looking at each other or thinking about anything. There is only one feeling and the force of it is such that they give up their memories and anxieties and are, at last, absolutely here.

Then they drink more wine, doze and wake together to have a rambling conversation in the dark in which they tell pure truths. Around midday they shower and get dressed (separately, demurely) but halfway down the stairs Raif touches Iris on the waist and they're back in the bedroom. They show each other what they want. Everything's new.

They spend the next five nights together, repeating and repeating themselves. Nothing lessens. On the third night, Iris has the dream she had as a child, about being made to see nothing, and she cries out. Raif, without waking, reaches a hand to cover her eyes. This is one of the most important things to happen to Iris and Raif and they sleep through it.

happiness

Here we are – so deep within ourselves that we feel nothing move. This is where love sleeps. We think it's something we build when it's waiting for the space we make.

When David sees Iris, whose name dissolves on his tongue, he feels his body become space and his surfaces grow strong. He has such a sense of capacity! He met a girl on a train and discovered that sitting down beside her made her feel alright. And now he can't tell people who she is. They see a woman in her late forties who has learnt to guard herself. He sees a creator of space and a builder of edges.

He never told her that her presence in his life made him happier than anything else and that he loved her with an ache because he knew the limits of her love for him. He knelt before her on their wedding night knowing that he was not the man for whom she'd left a life. They were never equal but for some years the power passed from one to the other without debate. Only while Iris grew into motherhood and her museum career, he got left behind, and the only way to stop himself disappearing was the blunt act of sex. He was looking for another woman on a different train. One who hadn't been rescued already.

Now David lives in a soft room. The bed billows, the chair too. There are spongy blocks and a drooping plastic table ledge attached by fuzzy bolts to the wall. He likes to sit at the table, picking up crayons and putting them down. As time goes by and he forgets what he wants, he will do less and less. He won't be able to think of anything he needs or wants to change or that doesn't happen already, and so will have no reason to act.

the unknown object

A meeting is called at the museum where it is announced that the stores are to be sold. They have been given seven years to prepare and as yet there is no confirmed destination. A property of such size is so valuable that nothing can justify its use but it is also protected and cannot be torn down. It will become another set of priceless rooms.

Iris and Max are asked to lead a team that will catalogue the non-accessioned items – all the unnumbered objects in the unopened boxes scattered throughout the stores. They'll spend the next seven years opening boxes with little or no idea of what's in them. Iris is thrilled.

It's like being young again and knowing nothing and hoping so much. Everything will be a surprise.

I know, says Max, but you're going to have to catalogue these surprises.

Despite all the care that's taken in numbering and cataloguing collections, every museum has objects that don't officially exist because they haven't yet been given a number. In the past this museum had far more money to make acquisitions than it had staff to evaluate objects. No one is sure but there are thought to be thousands of unnumbered items in the stores, many in boxes that have never been opened.

Iris places a box on a table. It is maybe fifty years old. This is a guess but an informed one. The name of the auction room scribbled on its side suggests that its contents are likely to be medical artefacts and so she must prepare for the hazards of asbestos, formaldehyde, lead paint and sharps.

She photographs every side of the box before she opens it and then photographs the packaging – a kind of wool she hasn't seen before. She lifts the object onto the table and photographs the number painted on its base. This could be given by an auction house, a hospital inventory or another museum. There's a second mark, very faint, which looks like a series of letters. She photographs that too. She'll add another number, for this museum, but it won't be permanent. The aim of every intervention now is that it can be undone.

The object has several components and each detachable part must be given its own number and photographed next to a card with that number written on it. There is an auction house slip, which Iris photographs as well as a torn tag, even though it is so tattered that it's unreadable. Both are placed in plastic envelopes. The twine that must have attached the label to the object is of particular interest to Iris as it is of a fibre she hasn't seen before. Unusual plant matter suggests overseas origins. She decides to send it for analysis if the object itself is important enough to justify the cost.

There is a growing interest among researchers and curators in the containers that the objects arrive in as well as those in which they're displayed. Some of the original glass cases from the galleries have been sent off for analysis and are about to become objects themselves. One day there will be a museum of containment that will contain nothing at all.

weakness allowed to remain

Iris decides that she must wait at least three months before introducing Raif to her daughters but the pressure of concealing him from them becomes too much. She starts to mention him, first as *a friend* who told her something interesting and then *my friend Raif* and then *Raif*. She mentions him while they're eating one evening and Lou rolls her eyes, which makes Kate giggle.

Mum, says Kate, can you talk about someone else?

Kate's twirling her fork in her pasta, staring at it rather than look at her mother. *She's embarrassed*, thinks Iris. *I am an embarrassment.*

What do you mean? she says. I talk about all my friends.

No you don't, says Kate.

Shut up, says Lou. It's her private life. It's private.

Iris is trying to process a number of things at once. That Lou and Kate are growing apart. That she assumed she could always tell what her girls felt and wanted but evidently hasn't been paying attention. That she is spoken of as *her*. There is so much to catch up with that she doesn't respond and the three of them sit there in a new kind of silence, carefully finishing their food.

A week later, Iris tells them that she has some news.

Is it Dad?

Is he dead?

He might have another stroke, says Kate. It says they usually do.

Mum, says Lou. Would you be sad if he did?

Listen. The thing is, I've started something with someone.

She means she's got a boyfriend, says Lou.

I know what she means.

Iris waits. She doesn't know how to begin.

I want to go and watch telly, says Kate.

Me too, says Lou, who is already on her way out of the room.

That night she can hear them shouting in their room and she stands on the stairs and listens.

But Iris is married!

It doesn't count! Not if David's—

David's what?

All the arguments she and David had in that house, thinking that if the door was closed the girls wouldn't hear them. They must have heard everything. When Lou comes in and slips into bed beside her, it is Iris who bursts into tears.

You don't have to meet him and I won't mention him again, not even his name. Nothing's going to change.

I've got pain, Mum.

I thought it was a good idea to say something but it made it sound as if it's a big deal and it's not and nothing will change.

Of course it will.

But you and Kate. It made you fight.

I'm tired, Mum. I've got pain.

I promise you . . . Where are you going?

To make myself a hot-water bottle.

When Lou tells Kate that Iris actually cried, they decide they should make her happy by asking to meet Raif. It's Iris's birthday and so they suggest he comes to tea. Iris has bought a cake and expects them to turn off the film they're watching and chat. He asks them about school and they offer brief polite responses while Iris finds it impossible to speak. Then Kate starts to ask questions.

Are you forty-eight too?

No, I'm almost forty-two.

Why haven't you got any children?

My wife was sick and then she died.

Was she like Mum?

She was from Estonia. It's a small country on the Baltic coast that used to be—

It was in the Cold War, says Lou. We did it at school.

She was in a war? asks Kate.

Not really. But it was a very difficult time.

Why?

Glad to have something to talk about, he explains what Liis's life had been like, and mentions her father and her trip to New York, and as he's doing this he remembers that he hasn't told Iris what he now knows. So he sticks to the story of her father defecting and the choice she had to make.

What was her name? asks Kate.

Liis Must.

He spells it.

Is she famous?

No.

But we could look her up.

I don't think there's anything. It was all such a long time ago.

Iris sees his discomfort and mistakes it for pain.

Why don't you watch the rest of your film? she says to the girls. We'll clear up.

In the kitchen he tells her about what Ava discovered and Iris just nods. She doesn't ask what it's done to him or why he couldn't tell her before. Nor does she urge him to probe the matter further. She leans against him and they sit there, shoulder to shoulder, not pretending to solve anything.

That night Kate and Lou do a search on Liis Must. Nothing that comes up is in English except for one article with a headline about a daughter's dilemma. They click on it but it's behind a paywall and at that moment a message pops up from one of Lou's friends with a picture of a boy and they forget all about their mother's friend, his dead wife and her war.

I like Raif, Lou tells Iris because she can see that her mother is worrying.

I like him too, says Kate. So can we stop talking about him now?

Raif was not the only person invited to Iris's birthday tea. The girls had phoned their grandmother Jean and left a message asking her to come down as a surprise. They'd looked up trains and could advise her on how best to cross the city. Lou left all the details in a careful, clear voice and they sent their love. Jean had not rung back. They knew not to tell Iris this and so it became, for Kate and Lou, one of those capsules of sadness that ought to dissolve but never do, something they were getting used to.

it won't change anything

Raif wants to talk about Iris too. He starts with his mother. They're sitting side by side on the sofa and she's picking as usual at a mark that isn't there.

I'm afraid it didn't work out with Helen.

Bridget nods carefully. Does she know Helen? Is this news good or bad?

I've met someone else, he says.

Bridget actually howls. These are words she's heard before and they have direct access to her heart. She has been wrenched back thirty years to her beloved husband turning over in bed, taking her face in his hands and saying, with horrifying tenderness, *I've met someone else.*

Raif does not know this.

It's nothing, he says, taking her hand. Nothing serious.

Met on a train, of all places! shouts Bridget. Someone else!

Not on a train, at a museum.

I know where you met!

It won't change anything, he says in desperation, and just like that, Bridget is calm.

He has hit on the words that thirty years ago calmed her. Her fists unclench and she turns to meet his eyes, wary of what she'll find there.

It won't change anything, she echoes.

Everything will be exactly the same.

He draws his mother towards him so as to comfort them both. He will not mention Iris for now.

Bridget will never understand who Iris is and Raif will never know about what happened between his parents forty years ago and how much this has to do with how he is formed. Determined not to pass on our pain, we carry it in ways that can be seen. It might become a great swelling in the throat, an adaptation in how we move, an inability to see or swallow.

When Raif tells the triplets about Iris, they immediately want to meet her. He suggests tea at the museum rather than at either home. Iris sees three cheeky little sprites who don't know how to be a grown-up version of themselves because there isn't one. She doesn't yet know that this is just who they are for Raif.

How old are you? asks Ashley.

Are you divorced? adds Emily. Or have you never been married?

You look married, puts in Jessica.

They're used to people being charmed by their rudeness. Raif finds it exhilarating. It paralysed Helen but provokes quite a different response in Iris.

I'm forty-eight, I have two daughters who are about to become nightmares. I have a husband who will live whatever time is left to him in a locked ward. I've got a mortgage and debt. I'm shorter and plainer-looking than you expected. I'm going to spend the next seven years unpacking boxes and packing them again because that is my job. I'm glad I've got one. I met Raif right here, in that doorway, and now we are where we are and who knows what that means. How old are you?

The triplets are insulted and then enchanted. For Raif it's as if Iris has stepped out from behind a wall. He hopes that getting close to her will entail more occasions like this.

sometimes we are in the same city

Iris and Raif leave the museum hand in hand – neither beautiful nor certain nor young. They move slowly, trailing their memories and gravities, weights and measures, categories and labels. We know how this works and what we bring.

I don't want to live with you, she says. And I don't want to marry you. I'm not doing those things again.

She probably will.

They have got far enough not to repeat themselves and they look at the past differently now – as all that has led to their beginning.

Do they understand that their capacity to go forward together comes from the very thing that's held them back? Repetition teaches us how to recognise our true nature as we're returned again and again to the aspects of ourselves that we cannot reshape. We learn how to say *I cannot do or be or live like this* and if we're lucky we also learn how to say *That is what makes me happy. I will pursue and cherish that.*

The past is always breaking down and rebuilding. And repetition, like memory, is never perfect: the original is always altered a little in the act. And the idea that two people can take up a line and feel its pull wherever they are is too simple. Life in the city is one of constant revision, diversion and impediment. Nothing proceeds straightforwardly. Lovers can only hope to find themselves in the same place and, if they're lucky, looking in the same direction.

They're there now, on the corner, waiting to cross. You can't see them from the hill or the seventy-second floor and you won't know them when they pass. But let them pass. Let them walk on into the afternoon. These will be their simplest days for some time to come.

Acknowledgements and sources

All of the objects mentioned in this book are in the Science Museum, London, and the Wellcome Trust's collections. I encountered most of them when the museum gave me their first artist's residency in 1995. I am grateful for their interest and support. I'm also grateful to the Wellcome Trust for the Engagement Fellowship which enabled me to pursue this work.

I am indebted to Paul Fletcher, Bernard Wolfe Professor of Health Neuroscience at the University of Cambridge, for conversations about everything from visual memory to disinhibition to metaphor, and to Dr Ruth Horry at the Wellcome Collection, who talked to me about objects and conservation, and introduced me to the copy of the Babylonian model of a sheep's liver. Thanks are also due to the conservator Jenny Mathiasson, formerly of the Whipple Museum of the History of Science. Their generosity, interest and insight have been invaluable.

The quotations in the section on the bone skate come from William Fitzstephen (1180), *Fitz-Stephen's Description of the City of London, translated by Samuel Pegge* (London: B. White, 1772). The balloonists' adventure related in that on the cloud mirror is drawn from James Glaisher, *Travels in the Air* (London: Bentley, 1871). The section on the wonder box includes lines from H. G. Wells, *Floor Games* (London: Frank Palmer, 1911). The section on the lancet includes a quote from 'The history and evolution of surgical instruments: VI The surgical blade: from fingernail to ultrasound', Dr John Kirkup, *Annals of the Royal College of Surgeons of England*, 1995; 77: 380–88.

The section on the jealousy glass includes a quote from *The Young Gentleman and Lady's Philosophy, in a continued survey of the works of nature and art; by way of dialogue*, Vol. II, Benjamin Martin (London: W. Owen, 1781).

The excerpt from 'Venus' by Malcolm Lowry is reprinted by permission of SLL/Sterling Lord Literistic, Inc. Copyright by the Estate of Malcolm Lowry.

I would like to thank Sarah Chalfant and Alba Ziegler-Bailey at the Wylie Agency, my copyeditor Silvia Crompton, my editor Mitzi Angel and all at Faber: Rachel Alexander, Kate Burton, Emmie Francis, Anne Owen and Jonny Pelham.

Thank you to my close readers, and thank you to my closest ones.